ABADDON'S EVE

Little
DOZEN
press

Abaddon's Eve

ABADDON'S EVE

BOOK 1 OF THE PROPHET TRILOGY

by Rachel Starr Thomson

Little Dozen Press

2015

CHAPTER 1

The voice of the wild man, the holy man, rising up out of the darkness, always gave Alack the shivers.

He was out there somewhere—down in the valley in the shadows beneath the moonlight. Eighteen-year-old Alack sat beneath the shelter of a twisted, wild fig tree, his woolen cloak pulled tightly around him. His sheep, bedded for the night, were quiet but for the occasional baa and the shuffling of their feet. The night was still, but warmth still emanated from the sands that had been heated by the desert sun only hours ago.

In the second watch of the night the wild man's cries had begun.

Alack's father, Naam, seated on the other side of their small fire, pushed pebbles aside with his staff and grunted.

"Why does he cry so, Father?" Alack asked. The old man, still strong, looked at him with wise eyes under wrinkled, heavy brows.

"He sees it coming," his father said.

The shiver took him again, more deeply this time. Stars overhead shone with a fierce knowing, a terrible, distant forbearance.

Somewhere down in the desert darkness the holy man howled at the sky, a cry of torment and suffering at the visions he saw and the truth he knew. Alack could picture him: tall, half-naked in his camel skins, his hair and beard uncut, his ribs standing out in a body that was thin but wiry and terrifyingly strong. Eyes roving and wild, but with the ability to pierce right through you.

But his tongue—oh, his tongue was like fire. When he spoke, everyone listened. They *flocked* to listen. They could not help it.

Those who heard his words shook in their sandals with fear, or else they mocked or debated; there could be no ignoring the man, no simply writing him off as crazy.

But it was more terrible still to hear his torments out here in the wilderness, with no one listening to his tongue of fire.

The sheep were beginning to bleat anxiously, perhaps mistaking the holy man's howls for those of a jackal. Alack rose to calm them, passing through the little flock, murmuring to them and laying his hands on their wooly heads and necks. Then he sank down on his haunches and leaned his head against one of the old matrons as though he were one of her lambs. There, surrounded by sandy wool and gentle, stupid faces, the young shepherd felt protected and safe.

Sheltered from the seeing eyes of the stars and from the cries of a man seized by vision.

———◆———

Morning three days later, and the holy man appeared by the well of Beer-Abba, ranting and striding to and fro, and crowds knotted around him—shepherds there to water their flocks and traders to water their camels, women carrying jars for their households and slaves doing the same. They left their jars and their animals alone and pressed in closer to hear what the holy man had to say.

RACHEL STARR THOMSON

His words were like poetry, painting a terrifying picture.

"It comes: a day of darkness and of shadows, a day of clouds and of thick darkness. They come: a great people and a strong; a terrible army out of the west: there have not ever been their like seen in all the earth, neither shall there be any the like after them! A fire devours before them, and behind them a flame burns; the land is as the gardens of God before them, and behind them is a desolate wilderness, yea, and *nothing* shall escape them."

The holy man paused, sweeping his burning eyes across the crowd, scorching one after another with that gaze. None escaped it, not man or woman or slave or shepherd.

Alack stood riveted to the spot, unable to move even so much as to tear his eyes away. This was always the way of it: the holy man fascinated and terrified him more than anything or anyone else on earth.

And his words. His warnings. So terrible, and yet so strange.

"They come: the terrible army out of the west! They shall run like mighty men; they shall climb the wall like men of war; and they shall march every one on in a straight path, every one in his place, and they shall not break their ranks: neither shall one wound another; they shall walk every one in his path, and when they fall upon the sword, they shall not be wounded. They shall run in the city; they shall run upon the wall, they shall climb upon the houses; they shall enter in at the windows like a thief."

The holy man's eyes lifted, and every gaze followed his. Up the mountain to the city on a hill: great Shalem, the Chosen City, shining like a sun in its beauty. Stone walls caught the light and reflected them; the spires of the temple rose beyond them, and the gold of the temple roof blazed with light. Bethabara, with its well and its market, was the last town on the way up the mountain to Shalem and owed all its prosperity to the city and the temple above. Shalem's doom would be their own.

The holy man's tone fell, from a trumpet call to the terrible finality of judgment. No one looked at him now; all eyes were fixed on the city above them.

"The earth shall quake before the army that is coming; the heavens shall tremble: the sun and the moon shall be dark, and the stars shall withdraw their shining. And the Great God shall utter his voice before his army: for he is strong who executes the Great God's word. For the day of the God is great and very terrible; and who can stand in it?"

Alack swallowed hard. In that moment even the animals fell silent.

But then the expected voice—the challenge that always came.

"Blasphemer," the voice said. "Naysayer. Fearmonger. Go back to the desert and preach your warnings to the locusts. We have nothing to fear from you."

"It is not I you should fear," the holy man said. "Not I, but the Great God himself who speaks these words against you."

"And for what cause?" the challenger said. By now eyes had shifted to the one who had interrupted: a familiar sight to all the townspeople. Aurelius Florus Laurentinus was the very antithesis of the holy man: broad-shouldered and muscular, dressed in fine clothes, well-groomed and clean. Light skin spoke of his foreign ancestry, from a land west of the Holy People, but his family had lived here for generations and earned the trust of many. And his voice, instead of bringing trembling and terror, brought calm—assurance. Even Alack felt better when Aurelius spoke.

"You all turned your eyes upon the Beloved City," Aurelius said, addressing the crowd. "Tell me, then; what did you see?"

"The glory of the sun," one man answered.

But Alack's mind returned the words of the holy man: *The sun and the moon will refuse to shine.*

"The temple spires," another said.

"The temple spires," Aurelius repeated. "The place where we worship the very God this lunatic threatens us with. What do you have to fear from the Great God's armies? You are the Great God's armies! You are his people. Shalem is his Chosen City. Have not all the prophets told you so? Does not our king sacrifice to the God of Gods at every festival and every holy day? This man with his words would subvert your hearts. He is the enemy of your prosperity and the enemy of your peace. You would all do well to ignore him—let him rant out his predictions to himself alone."

Alack thought of the howls rising from the darkened valley, and his heart pained him. There was cruelty to Aurelius's scorn. Such a lonely, anguished cry as this man's Alack had never heard; at the very least, should not one listen to him out of compassion?

"Go back to your herds, back to your work," Aurelius said, and the crowds turned to obey him. He was after all the chief man of the town, the king's voice among the people; if Aurelius the Governor said they were fools, they most likely were. Alack wondered if the holy man would be angry that they were all turning their backs. That he himself was turning his back—that his feet were carrying him back to his flock as Aurelius told them to do.

He had turned away, just so, many times before.

But this time he could not. This time he could not rid himself of the man's cries in the darkness. And so he turned back and looked into the prophet's eyes.

And when their gazes met, Alack saw it.

A terrible army marching shield to shield, covering the valleys on every side, so numerous that the ground could not be seen, and the mountain shook with their coming . . .

Aurelius remained at the well until he was satisfied that the last of the townspeople had moved on, back to work and away from the troublemaking prophet. He glared at the shepherd boy, Alack, who seemed overinterested in the man; the boy turned his head, saw Aurelius's eyes boring into him, and shuffled away with his cheeks flushed. Good. Let him be embarrassed—let him be mortified that he had been seen listening to the mocker.

The prophet himself had ceased his ranting and simply stood watching as the people turned their backs and returned to their work, ignoring him. At last he shook his shaggy head as if in sorrow and despair, and he turned back to the desert with his bony shoulders hunched.

Aurelius spat in the dirt behind him. Had any governor ever suffered such trouble? And so close to the Holy City! Truly, this people was bold and stubborn. A pox on all who were forced to deal with them. But stubborn or no, they were not a people that he, and his fathers before him, could not outwit.

Aurelius turned and began the trek to his great house, his guards following him at a respectful distance. When his great-grandfather had first come to this land from the west, no one could have guessed that the foreigner would become ruler, that the stranger would govern the children of the land. But the first Aurelius was a crafty man with a golden tongue and a brave spirit, and when he had saved the life of a king's advisor in battle, the family's journey had been set. From there Aurelius's grandfather, Marcus, had worked his way into the royal courts, and his father, also called Marcus, had become a friend of the king.

Aurelius himself cared less for the courts of the king and more for a position where he could rule, and so he had convinced the king to make him governor of this, Bethabara, the closest and most important of the towns on the ascent to the Chosen City. Every third month he returned to Shalem, where he had the ear of the king, and then he came back to Bethabara where none challenged his wisdom or authority.

None but the mad prophet.

But this had always been a land of mad prophets and unstable religionists. A far cry from the ways of his forefathers. He remembered his grandfather's stories of the land to the north and west, on the Great Sea, where every man worshipped any god he fancied, with no threats of jealous retribution from the God of the Mountain.

It was true—the stories these people told had raised fear and awe even from Aurelius when he was a boy. But now he saw them as foolishness. What sort of supreme god entrusted his messages to half-mad wanderers in the wilderness? In any case, the king was faithful to placate the Great God. There would be no judgment, no revenge. Revenge for what, after all? The king slaughtered enough sheep and bulls and shed enough blood to satisfy the most voracious of spirits.

Bethabara was built on the sides of the mountain, and the street sloped sharply up as Aurelius climbed to his house. Built of shining limestone, it was the finest structure in the town; glowing with light in the morning and evening as the rising lights of day and night reflected upon it. Its gates were of high, finely wrought brass, and Aurelius's guards called for them to be opened as they approached.

He passed through the gate into the courtyard, where a fountain gushed cool water and olive trees lent their shade over hard-packed earth. His wife, seated on a bench with a harp in her hand, rose to greet him. Marah was a beautiful woman, daughter of one of the old families of Shalem, stately and crafty and every bit Aurelius's match. He loved her at times and hated her at others, but life alongside her was never dull.

She went to kiss his cheek and whispered in his ear, "She is here."

"So soon?" he murmured back. He let his eyes wander now and took in the clear signs of recent arrivals. Hoofprints had stirred up the dirt of the courtyard; the beasts had left refuse that had yet to be cleaned up. "I would her journey had been a little slower," he said. "The prophet is in the town."

His wife stepped back and gave him a disdainful look. "You should have him beaten and run out."

"The king does not like unnecessary dramatics. Especially not toward one who claims to speak for the Great God."

"Outdated sentiment."

"Perhaps, but you know these people. Their superstitions die hard."

"As do your sister's."

He cursed inwardly. How had she taken her journey so fast? He had not expected her for another day at least.

"I must see her, mustn't I?" he said.

"Indeed you must. She insists on seeing you at the nearest opportunity. I urged her take her time about cleaning up, but you know Flora—she considers herself already as clean as need be."

Aurelius sighed and patted his wife's arms before releasing her. "You ought to help me be more charitable toward her, not antagonize me."

"As if you need more antagonizing."

If his foreign heritage was Aurelius's greatest overcoming and his position at court his greatest pride, his half-sister was the thorn in the garden of his triumphs. Flora approached life as though their forefathers had not accomplished anything in becoming favoured in this land, as though all their privileges were worth less than the sands of the desert surrounding them. A desert where she had chosen to spend most of her life in a community of fanatics, mercifully far away from him. His mother had disliked Flora with a passion, little surprise given her origin as the daughter of a whore their father liked too well, and had sometimes muttered that she wished Marcus had enacted the ancient rights of his ancestors and exposed the girl while she was in infancy.

That had not happened, and Flora was alive, well, and far too wealthy and privileged to be anything but trouble.

Aurelius had not turned to go into the house before her voice accosted him from the door, and he turned with a smile plastered on his face to greet her.

"My brother is here at last," she said. "And why were you not here to meet me?"

"You are early, dear sister," he called across the courtyard, spreading out his arms to embrace her. "You might have sent word that you drew close."

"Ah, but then I would not have the pleasure of seeing your surprise," Flora said, pecking him on the cheek.

Flora Laurentii *Infortunatia* was a strikingly beautiful woman. Aurelius's wife paled before her, a fact which was not lost on Marah. Tall and statuesque, with thick black hair that waved and curled down her back and eyes of a striking green, Flora favoured her mother and made it clear to any who would possibly wonder why Marcus had gone astray. She had been married at thirteen and promptly outlived that husband, who was carried away by an unexpected stroke only two years after their marriage; then married again and widowed within a fortnight by an unfortunate accident in the streets. By that time she had a reputation, and no one came seeking her hand, and she had as well a small fortune, left her by the second husband.

She was also a raving, wild religious fanatic whose pronouncements and self-abasement Aurelius hated almost as much as the words and actions of the prophet.

With the eyes of his wife and all the servants and guards in the courtyard upon him, Aurelius embraced his sister for exactly as long as politeness required and then stepped back and took her arm to usher her back inside.

Better just to keep her away from everyone as much as possible. He shuddered to think what sort of trouble she was likely to cause him this time.

"Was your journey pleasant?" he asked as they entered the house.

"As pleasant as a desert trek ever may be," Flora answered.

"And you will stay with us for a fortnight, I presume? On your way to the Holy City?"

Something flashed across her face—something that gave him heartburn just to witness.

"The 'Holy City,' as you call it, has no fascination for me. I would as soon visit a rotting dog. No, Brother, I thought I would remain here until my business is done. Word has been sent to my business partners to attend me in your house."

He blanched. "And you expect all of that will take . . ."

"From one moon to the next, if all goes well." She stopped and smiled coyly at him, a smile so beautiful and so beguiling that most men would have lost their knees at the sight. "But you needn't pretend that news is pleasant to you, Brother. Rest assured I shall not take a day longer about my business than is required."

He felt his body going as stiff as his voice. "That is hardly necessary, Flora."

"Neither are lies. I know that you suffer me because you have to, and because you know you will receive something from my estate when I die. Fair enough, dear brother. Your reward cometh in its own good time, and for now, I require nothing more than that you house me and feed me once a year while I conduct business and grow the fortune that shall in part pass to you."

He groped for words. In all these years of tacit understanding, and all of the effort he had put into pretension that she saw right through, she had never come out and stated the game quite so plainly.

She was in a mood, then. This was likely to be the worst visit yet.

"Will you require anything special during your stay?" he asked.

"Only a place where I may receive my guests. You have rooms you can give me, I know. And while I am not conducting business, your forebearance."

She gave him a pointed look with her devastating green eyes. He knew what she meant.

"We will not interfere with your worship."

Her expression grew more tender, less combative. "I wish you would give me more than forebearance, Aurelius. I wish you would *listen* to me. You call trouble on this house and your heads by scorning the Great God."

"We do not scorn him," Aurelius said stiffly; "we are strangers and owe him nothing, yet we visit the temple and offer sacrifices like the People of the land."

"You live on *his* land; you owe him everything. And the sacrifices offered at the temple are an abomination. The Great God requires justice, and the priests give him bribes instead. You do not give him what he *wants*, Aurelius. The People are blind and deaf, shutting out his prophets—"

She saw something in his face, and zeroed in. "His prophets. Aurelius, the prophet is here. Yes, he is, and I see it in your face. Have you invited him into your house?"

"Of course not," he snapped. "The man is mad. I commanded the people to turn their backs on him and return to their work; he was stirring up a crowd again. I tell you, if the people are not shepherded it will cause trouble for all of us. Even you, Flora, while you are with us."

She looked sad. That was what drove him most beside himself about her. The ranting and raving and fanatical piety and cloistered life in the desert he could handle, but her sincerity made him want to do violence to someone or something. That sadness in her eyes. She'd been looking at him like that since they were little more than children and she had become a devoted follower of the Great God of the People and he had remained as their fathers had been—practical, nostalgic about their homeland, and determined to rise in the world the only way anyone could. Through good sense and pragmatism, especially in matters of gods and men.

"If the prophet is here, I must see him," Flora continued.

"Not here," he said sharply. "You may receive any businessman you like in my courtyard, but the prophet does not enter my house. Is that understood?"

She stuck out her chin stubbornly. "Then I will go out to him, wherever he may be."

Aurelius groaned. Flora *would* go, and she would attract the attention of the entire town, as she always did. And all the people of Bethabara would know that their governor's sister went out to consort with the prophet.

He could only hope they would all recognize her for the lunatic she was and avoid being swayed by her example.

He only wished that was likely.

CHAPTER 2

A lack could not shut the vision out of his head. He had seen it. The terrible army of the prophet's warnings, marching upon them with death and destruction in the dust of their feet. The vision burned in his eyes. He would tell his father and ask his advice. As the crowd dispersed at Aurelius's command, he sought his father with his eyes—

But they fell on Rechab instead, and so his purpose was diverted. He had not known she was back, and his heart leaped at the sight of her. He pressed through the crowd, edging and elbowing his way to the well and her side.

She did not see him at first. Her eyes were on the prophet, watching as the man trudged back out toward the desert.

"Rechab," he said, his voice catching.

She turned, light leaping up in her soft brown eyes. "Alack!"

He drank in the sight of her. Small and feminine; clothed in home-spun; her dark hair tied back except for a few curls that had fought loose and hung around her face and neck. Rechab was startlingly beautiful by any standard, but it was her eyes that drew him most. Eyes that spoke of laughter and secrets and childhood, and at the same time of mystery and growing up—of love.

That vision, of the face he loved and dreamed of most, temporarily drove out the terrible marching of the prophet's armies.

"When did you return?" he asked.

"Only just now . . . the journey has been long."

"But you are back now," he said. "Back for the autumn."

Her face fell. "Alack, things are different now . . ."

"You cannot be going out again so soon!"

"My father says trade is good. The nomads brought him riches; he wants to take them to the Holy City in just a few days."

"But . . . you do not have to go with him . . ."

She sighed. "You know I would stay if I could, Alack."

He swallowed hard. He knew the words she was not saying. That if he were less a boy and more a man, if he could put down the bride price, she would stay. Then they would not just be children playing at love; they would be betrothed, with a future.

A future that would never come.

Shepherd boys did not rate high on any tradesman's list of hopeful sons-in-law. Especially not dirt-poor shepherd boys with nothing of their own to offer.

She reached out and touched his arm, filling him with the tremulous desire to rise up and fight someone, something, for her.

"But it will not be a long journey, Alack. My father will go and trade and we will come back."

"Rechab, I—"

"Shhh." Her eyes pleaded with him. "You know it is no good to speak words to me when we cannot act on them."

"I am saving. I have saved . . ."

"Alack." For the first time he realized she looked sadder, older, than usual. It had been three months since she last sat and talked with him in Bethabara, and whatever had transpired in that time had changed her.

Or perhaps it was only time itself that had changed her.

She looked away from him and began to turn her back. "I must return to my father."

"Can I come and see you? Before you leave?"

She hesitated.

She was going to say no.

His heart plummeted.

But she said, "Yes. In the usual place. But only for a few minutes. My father grows more watchful of me, Alack. He is starting to grow jealous."

"I will come tonight."

She smiled. "I will wait for you."

Then she was gone. He watched her weave into the crowd. To most eyes she would have disappeared in the mass of bodies and homespun cloth, sinew and sandals, but not to his. He knew where she was until she had disappeared into the narrow streets of the town.

His father cleared his throat. He jumped. He had been so fixed on following Rechab's progress that he did not notice the old man's approach.

"She is a beautiful girl," Naam said.

Alack swallowed, terrified.

"Your mother was a beautiful woman."

"Why are you saying that?"

"Because I understand. But Alack, you are just a boy. And you will never marry Rechab."

He hated those words.

He had heard them in his own mind and heart ten thousand times, but he had never told his father about his feelings for his playmate, because he never, ever wanted to hear them spoken aloud.

"There is a price to be paid," his father went on, "and you cannot afford it."

"I am saving . . ."

"Her father will never accept a price you can afford, my son. Not if you save your shekels for forty years. And Rechab will not wait forty years."

Word after word, truth after truth, that he had been avoiding hearing since the day he decided he loved Rechab. Two years ago.

But he was shocked to see tears in his father's old eyes when he turned around to look at him.

Naam put a hand on his son's shoulder. "I am sorry, my boy. I hoped you would not dream. But I always knew it was a foolish hope."

Alack looked back up the street where Rechab had disappeared.

It was all true.

She would never be able to wait for him to save enough to afford the price her father set. Not because she would not. But because she would not be allowed to wait. Some girls had a say in who they wanted to marry, because their fathers listened to their wishes. Rechab did not, because her father did not.

"Come, Alack," Naam said. "It is back to the hillside we must go."

Casting one last look over his shoulder, Alack turned and followed his father back to the sheep.

RACHEL STARR THOMSON

Rechab lifted a jug of water to her shoulder and began the trek back home thoughtfully. Her heart ached over Alack. Her childhood friend—closer than a brother. Her household had never been a friendly place; her mother had died giving birth to her, and Rechab's older sisters and brothers—six of them—were both considerably older and somewhat resentful of her. They were all married now, and gone. Her father, Nadab the Trader, was as mercenary a man as was ever born in the land, and as Rechab represented little more to him than a future dowry, he cared for her as one would for a piece of merchandise. As it became clearer that she would grow to be the most beautiful of his four daughters, he took special care to keep her fed, protected, and somewhat educated. She'd long felt like a sheep being fattened for slaughter.

Into the vacuity of her home life had come Alack, a boy from whose flocks her father sometimes purchased sheep, and she loved him. She'd always loved him. And she'd always known their love was doomed.

The hope in his eyes broke her heart now. Why hadn't he known the same thing? Why hadn't he guarded himself better, innocuated himself like she had with a lifetime of proclaiming internally that it was all very well to love a friend, but that love could never, ever transition to marriage?

If Alack could find a way to transform himself from shepherd to prince, or to transfer to himself the wealth of a great merchantman, then it might be possible. But not otherwise. And since that would surely never happen, the sooner he disenchanted himself with her, the better.

Truly, that was what hurt the most. The idea that Alack would do what he had to do—cut her out of his heart and leave her alone in the world.

A commotion in the streets drew her attention, and she stopped and turned to see a woman going by, on foot, with a large entourage of guards and servants that spoke greater wealth than her conveyance suggested. They seemed to be headed for the well.

Rechab watched them go and then took up her own journey again. She wondered why a woman of such obvious means went to the well at all—why not just send servants for water?

She must be going to see the prophet.

Thought of the prophet sent a shudder through Rechab's small frame. His appearance repelled her; his words terrified her. And yet, like all others in the town, she could not help being drawn to hear him.

And unlike most others in the town, she found no assurance in Aurelius's brave words. He promised the people that Shalem, the Holy City, was their protection and strength. But she had spent the last year journeying to the Holy City with her father, and she knew there could be no protection from the Great God there. Something in Shalem was terribly wrong—something dark lurked in its shadows. It plagued her sleep and woke her in terror. The thought that the prophet's words might come true, and a terrible army would raze the Holy City to the ground—

She found comfort in them.

Wrestling her thoughts away from the darkness and the prophet and her own nightmares, Rechab forced her feet off the main street and up a narrow side path to her father's home, a house nearly as impressive as Aurelius's. But where the governor had been installed in riches due to his favour at court, her father had earned every penny of his. Shrewd and calculating he might be, but his dealings were ultimately honest and his riches gained through merchandise, not through politics or thievery.

Rechab passed the servant women baking flat bread in the round ovens in the yard and set her pot of water in a line with other pots, ready for use. A private cistern, behind the line of pots, was covered to keep its precious store safe. Nadab's household made use of the well Beer-Abba like everyone else did, reserving the cistern for times of need.

The afternoon passed in chores and conversations with the servants as she ensured the household ran smoothly and efficiently. She had stepped into the role of lady of the house at the age of fourteen and did it now with hardly an extra thought. Her absence over the last year had necessitated the house servants taking greater charge, and there were one or two she trusted implicitly. So in the busywork of the day there was little to draw her attention away from the fact that Alack was coming, and that her heart ached for him.

Over supper her father announced, "I suppose you will be seeing that shepherd boy soon."

She looked up, startled. Nadab's eyes bored into her, and he nodded as though he saw what he was looking for. Dipping his bread in olive oil, he went on without glancing at her again.

"I expect you to conduct yourself as becomes your position in my house."

"Yes, Father, of course. I . . ."

"I do not object to a visit from a childhood friend. But you must also keep in mind that you are not a child."

She looked down at her food. "Yes."

"Which brings me to another thing. The way you dress."

She frowned. "My dress . . ."

"I saw you coming back from the well; you looked like a peasant."

Her back stiffened. "I can hardly wear finery to the well, Father."

"In that case I think you should not continue to go to the well."

She sought for words. "I have always done my share of work. You trust the household to me—"

"Then you can stay here and manage it, like my wife would do if I had a wife. You are a woman, Rechab, and one who will fetch a high price. I do not want you lessening your value in anyone's eyes because you act or look like a servant."

She took a moment, fighting to digest what he was saying. Diminish her value in whose eyes? What did it matter what the people of this town, where she had been born and raised, thought of her? They all knew exactly who she was and exactly what her life was. Acting like a high-born woman of the city would only make her look arrogant.

She nearly said all that, but in the moments between formulating her objections and voicing them she realized the problem wasn't with the townspeople at all: her father had his sights on a son-in-law, or perhaps several possibilities, and they came from the city. He wanted her accustomed to looking like a high-born woman because those who would be looking at her would expect that. Perhaps one of them would even journey here, and then he was not to see his future wife "devalued" by carrying water.

She wanted to groan, to hide her face, to rush out of the room.

Or to say, "Please, Father, do not marry me to a man from the city. I cannot live in Shalem. I can hardly bear to visit that place. Do as you always planned to do and marry me to a desert merchant; they have money aplenty, and I can live a nomad's life. I cannot live in Shalem."

None of the words would come out.

"You look pale," Nadab said.

She raised her eyes to him, willing herself to take courage. But what good would it do? Her father would not listen.

"I hear your wishes," was all she said. "And I will obey."

A moment later his attention had shifted to a platter of figs and honeyed cakes. He did not bother to offer her any, and she could not face the idea of eating anyway.

In the dark behind the house an hour later, she shivered as she waited for Alack to come.

The air was not cold.

It was the thoughts of Shalem that chilled her.

Of living there.

Becoming one of its own.

Being sucked down into the darkness that dwelt beneath the shining temple roof.

"Rechab?" his voice said, startling her so badly she jumped. "Rechab, I'm sorry. It's me."

"I know. I know." She attempted a smile and knew it was weak. Chances were he could not see it in the darkness anyway. The moon was bright tonight, but its light did not penetrate the shadows where she hid. "I was only lost in thought."

"Then I am glad I found you," he said with a smile she could hear. "Won't you come into the moonlight?"

She shook her head. "No. No, I like the shadows tonight."

"Is it the prophet's words that are bothering you?"

It was not—she had hardly thought of them again after leaving the well—but she said, "Yes. Perhaps it is that."

He was quiet an unusually long time. Then he said, "I saw it."

She waited for him to explain.

He picked up his words again, picking up courage with them. "I saw the vision. I looked into the prophet's eyes before he turned around, before Aurelius chased him off. And I saw an army coming. A great army, covering the whole wilderness like locusts and filling the air with dust like smoke. They marched as one, their shields joined, as though the whole mass of men was covered in a single piece of armour. Should such an army come, we will never stand against them. They will tear down the Holy City itself."

Good, she thought.

But she said, "My father says the prophet is a madman. Aurelius says the same."

"I don't think he is mad," Alack said.

She stirred, moving so she could see him a little better. He had not quite joined her in the shadows, and she could make out the outline of his face—an unremarkable face, really. Not strong or unusually handsome in any way. But one she knew and loved.

"I can hear him, out in the desert when I am tending the sheep. Sometimes at night he howls like a jackel and weeps. But I don't think he is crazy. His howling is that of a man in deep pain and grief. I think what he sees moves him to anguish." He paused. "So he must see more clearly than I do. I saw the vision, and it frightened me, but I do not feel his torment. I don't know why."

"Did you see a woman going after him?" Rechab asked. "A foreigner?"

"Yes; Aurelius's sister," Alack said.

"Truly?"

"So she said. She called herself Flora Laurentii."

"Ah," Rechab said, enlightened. "She is here?"

"She came this morning. They say she will stay here instead of going on to Shalem. I think Aurelius must be very angry about that."

They laughed. Stories of the governor's sister were legend, though she had rarely stayed more than a single night in Bethabara on her way to the city. Rechab had never seen her before. But the woman she had seen in the street certainly matched the description: breathtakingly beautiful, foreign, wealthy, and determined. All of that, and seeking out the mad prophet for a private audience.

Rechab felt a twinge of envy. To be free as Flora was! Even if the whole town said the woman was cursed, she could order her own destiny and direct her own paths. Surely that was worth a tarnished reputation and the wrath of a brother or two.

"What did she say to him?" Rechab asked, curious.

"To the prophet?"

"Yes."

"I don't know. She overtook him on the slope below the town, but they were too far off to hear. She did not speak with him long."

"Strange," Rechab said. "She seemed so determined to reach him. I would have thought they—"

She stopped as they both heard the sound of someone moving in the streets.

At this time of night it was not common for anyone to be out. The darkness was deep over the town, and night was not safe. But unmistakably, someone was in the street. Alack caught her eye and an instant later disappeared.

She followed him.

They circled the house and hunkered down together in the shadows where they had a clear view of the street and the man who had just passed. The outline of his body was clear against the moonlight. Tall, almost emaciated, and yet with an aura of strength. In the darkess the man's clothing looked like rags, and his hair was a wild cloud around his head.

The prophet.

The prophet had left the wilderness and come into the town.

Had he ever come so far in before?

Rechab looked up and met Alack's questioning glance in the moonlight. She nodded just slightly.

And followed Alack's lead as he vacated their place and crept into the street to trail the man. Her heart raced with excitement as they tiptoed along behind him, fifty paces back and not hidden. If he turned, he would see them.

But he did not turn.

They followed him through the tight streets until they reached the main road, and from there turned toward Aurelius's house.

The governor's house sat at the highest point of the town, up the slope that led eventually to Shalem. Its limestone walls shone in the moonlight like the Holy City's temple shone in the sun. Its guarded gates of brass opened only at the command of their master.

They watched incredulously as the gates opened and the prophet passed through.

"Come," Alack said, and he broke into a run.

Rechab went after him.

Together, they slipped through the still-open gates of the governor's house, following after the prophet.

CHAPTER 3

Oil lamps burned in the room of the governor's house where Flora Laurentii Infortunatia had set up her receiving area. No doubt Aurelius had intended it to be used during the day, but this guest was better received at night when no one, including the master of the house, would see him come or go.

The tall, gaunt man stood between the tall lampstands, his hollow cheeks shadowed in the flickering light, his eyes deep and shining—stars in a vast night sky. His arms folded, he watched her as she paced, taking in the sight of him before speaking.

At last she said, "Do you know me, Prophet?"

"You are the governor's sister."

"That is not what I meant. Do you know me?"

He nearly smiled at that. "Yes."

She nodded, satisfied. "I thought you did. I am gratified."

"The Great God does not overlook those who seek him. You seek him more fervently than most, though you are a stranger."

"I am twice a stranger," she said, speaking the words almost as if she were proud of them. "My father came from the western sea and my mother from the Hill People—one of the cursed people. My father's family worshipped gods of their own making, and my mother's the daemons of the mountains. And yet my heart burns to know the Great and True, and he has not struck me down for my seeking."

"No, indeed. He honours all who honour him. Even those whose families are strangers and rebels for generations."

She smiled. "So you know me. And I wish to know you. Who are you? They call you a wild man—the Mad Prophet. They never say your name."

"My name is lost in the Great God. Lost in my visions."

"But you have one." She peered intently at him, ceasing her pacing. "I have learned many things in my years of seeking, Prophet. Many riddles and wise sayings. So here is one wise saying I know to be true: One does not lose his name in the Great God, one finds it."

"My name is Kol Abaddon," the prophet said.

"Voice of Destruction."

"The same."

"You are still speaking in riddles."

"Until my visions come to pass, they consume me. I can have no identity, no name, outside of them. I give voice to them, and that is all."

Sadness graced her expression. "That is terrible," she said.

"I serve a terrible God."

"Certainly one who gives you terrible visions."

"Yes."

"That is the real reason I asked you to come. I want to know what you have seen." She motioned to a low chair. "Please, sit."

He looked behind him, uncomfortable. "I am not accustomed to chairs."

"But I am, so you will have to accommodate me. This is another wise saying: When you are a guest in a house, do as your host does."

He sat and said, "That is not always a wise saying."

"But it will do for now." She sat across from him, bathed in light, and leaned forward with an intense expression. "I must know what you have seen."

"A great army," he told her. "Marching on the land. It is the army of the Great God. Never have we seen a people like it—they march shield to shield, spear to spear, sword to sword, like a single body. They swarm the land like locusts. They will climb the walls of the Holy City and enter in at the windows, and the city will be utterly destroyed."

His eyes as he spoke were haunted, tormented. She knew he saw the words as he voiced them. This destruction was no mere theory, but a reality in which he lived every waking moment—and probably every sleeping moment too.

"Every year since I was widowed I have gone to conduct trade in the Holy City," Flora answered. "But this year I will not go up. I cannot continue to walk amidst the abominations there. Have you seen them, friend?"

Her address seemed to move him somehow; it took him a moment to answer her. "No. Only in vision. I have lived in the wilderness forty years."

She closed her eyes for a moment. "Forty. And I think of myself as devoted."

"As you should," the prophet said. "For you are. You, with your wise sayings, should know better than to compare yourself."

She smiled, though the pain did not leave her face. "Well said.

But back to the Holy City. It is a cesspool. A haunt of daemons. The temple itself is defiled, so they tell me—though I cannot go beyond the outer courts."

"That surprises me."

"That they will not let me in? I would not enter even if they would— I know the Great God's laws and honour them even if the People do not. I have no right to his sanctuary, with the blood that flows in my veins. But they still bar the inner courts from any but the People. In this one respect they hold true to the law. But in all others—my friend, they say an idol stands in the Holiest Place, and sacrifices are made to it on the Great God's altar. And all around the temple are shrines and grottos where other gods are worshipped. Worse, there is a darkness—"

She stopped and searched for words. "A darkness I can neither explain nor understand. But I feel it. It has grown with every passing year, until now I cannot enter the city at all without dread. Can you explain to me what I feel there?"

He frowned. "I do not know. You may feel the wrath of the Great God himself."

"Yet I think that would feel holy. And this does not. It is an evil."

"Then perhaps some spirit has taken up residence there. Certainly the People have opened the doors." Pain twisted his face. "You asked my name, and I told you it is lost. My past also is lost. But I will tell you this: the Holy City was once my home. The words you speak to me grieve me. But the sooner the city is destroyed, the better it will be for all the earth. Evil cannot remain unchallenged, and justice cannot be passed over forever. The wicked will be destroyed, though they should seat themselves in the most beloved garden of the universe."

"Thank you," Flora answered, "you have given me much to think about. Now, the other reason I called you here. I want to offer you my services."

His bushy eyebrows shot up. "My lady?"

She waved her hand. "Please, do not call me that. In this life I am the daughter of a whore, the curse-slayer of husbands, and the favourite of all gossips and scorners; you owe me no more than the honour given a merchantwoman. And in the spirit, I am a foreigner and a seeker. But yes, I offer you my services—in any way that I can be of help to you. I have servants, and guards, and money. Anything I can do for you, I beg you to tell me what it is."

"I have no needs," he said. He stood and laid a sudden and unexpected hand on her head.

"I bless you in the name of the Great God," he said. "You are wrong, Flora Laurentii—I will not call you Infortunatia—to account yourself as nothing. You are far more than you have said."

He lowered his hand, and she stared up at him for a moment before saying, "But you are also wrong, Kol Abaddon the Prophet. For I think you do have needs. And when I discover them, would God I may be the means to meet them."

She stood and held up a hand. "Now. You two who are lurking in the shadows, come out."

There was a long silence. And then shuffling feet, and the shadows revealed a boy and a girl, both on the verge of adulthood, dressed like peasants and holding hands. Both appeared deeply embarrassed.

"Look up and meet my eyes," Flora commanded. They did. She looked from one to the other and then said to the prophet, "Have you anything to say of these two?"

"The boy sees visions," the prophet said. "He sees my vision and hears my voice. I know you, Alack son of Naam the shepherd. Today was not the first time I have laid eyes on your face."

"And you," Flora said, tipping the girl's chin up. "Who are you?"

"I am called Rechab," the girl said, her voice quivering. "I am the daughter of Nadab the Trader."

"And you want to say something to me," Flora said. "That is how I knew you were there—I heard you gasp when I spoke of the Holy City."

"I have felt it too," Rechab said, her words rushing out. "The darkness you spoke of. My father takes me to the city with him when he trades; I cannot be there except I am plagued by nightmares and fear."

"Hmm," Flora said. She released the girl's chin and stepped back. "And now you are here with us. Why?"

"We followed the prophet," Alack said. "We saw him in the street."

Flora smiled. "You were out together at night?"

Rechab flushed. "Nothing untoward was happening."

Flora's smile disappeared; she saw something in the girl's face that spoke of heartache and injustice. Of course—the boy was clearly poor. The girl, though dressed like the peasantry, was a trader's daughter, and carried herself like one from a higher class. The story told itself.

Poor children, she thought.

But then—

This meeting was no chance accident. They were here for a reason.

Flora made up her mind in that moment to help these children somehow. After all, the boy was a budding prophet. And the girl had a heart that kicked against the dark spirit in Shalem. They were both of her own kind: the kind that sought the Great God, rebelled against the darkness, and invited trouble into their lives.

What she could do for them, she did not know. But she would help. Somehow.

"We must go," Rechab was saying. "My father may miss me, and I cannot be found to have been outside of the boundaries of his house with . . . with Alack."

"No, indeed," Flora said. "Nor, I suspect, would he be happy to know you have been meeting with the prophet?"

"It is true," Rechab said, looking away.

"Do not look ashamed at that. This meeting is held in darkness because if my brother knew who was in his house, he might throw us all out." Flora reached out again and touched the girl's face, making her look at her. "I will tell you another wise saying: In times such as these, he who seeks the Great God invites great trouble. But with the trouble comes great reward. You remember that."

Rechab nodded and forced a smile. "We must go," she repeated.

"You must," Flora agreed. "And so . . ." She turned, about to address the prophet.

But only Alack stood there. He shrugged.

The prophet was already gone.

⸻ ⟡ ⸻

Rechab awoke early and started about her chores before the first light of dawn. To please her father she dressed herself in finer clothes than usual, veiled her face and wore earrings of silver, and went into the market to haggle for the day's allotment of fresh fruit and corn.

When she returned to the house midmorning, she was so startled to hear the voice emanating from her father's reception room that she nearly dropped the basket of melons she was carrying.

It was Flora.

She could not make out the words, but the imperious and determined tone was unmistakable. As was her father's mix of annoyance and admiration. Nadab had always appreciated anyone who would stand up to him and drive a hard bargain; Flora might be a woman and unusual, but the novelty of being faced by such a one might only heighten Nadab's admiration in the end. Rechab set down her basket and lingered by the door, which burst open only moments later. Her father's enormous form stood in the doorway.

"Rechab!" he bellowed.

"I am here, Father," she said.

"Rechab, come inside. There is a most unusual woman here with a most unusual request."

Rechab entered as commanded. The sight of her visitor took her breath away. Flora had come in state. She wore silks dyed purple and scarlet and a veil of linen so fine as to be transparent. Golden bracelets encircled her wrists, six on either hand, and earrings of gold called attention to the striking beauty of her green eyes. She might have been a goddess, Rechab thought. No wonder her father admired her—as clearly he did. Her presence was awe-inspiring, and Rechab wondered that she had stood in the same room with this woman and talked with her face-to-face just last night, without ceremony or fear.

Flora's face betrayed no recognition now, although Rechab thought she saw a twinkle in her eyes. She stood still as Flora looked her over with a haughty air.

"Yes, she'll do nicely," Flora said, turning her head back to Nadab. "I trust you can afford to dress her a little more appropriately?"

"Of course," Nadab said, shooting his daughter a look that "I told you so."

"Then I am well pleased. Girl, your father says you are trained to deal with merchants and hold your head up proudly. Can you do that?"

"Yes," Rechab stammered.

"Convince me," Flora said.

Rechab straightened her shoulders and steadied her voice. "Yes."

"Look me in the eye."

Rechab did. There it was—an unmistakable twinkle. A promise.

Her heart leaped at the sight of it.

This woman might be intimidating in every respect, but she was a friend, and she had come here as a friend.

Rechab didn't think her father could see that. The look in Flora's eye was strictly a two-way communication.

She kept her gaze, and with shoulders still straight and her tone easy, she said, "Yes, I can do as you say. You wish me to represent you?"

Flora smiled now, and the smile took in Nadab as though to say she was thrilled with him. "The very thing. I am in this town to do business with merchants from the desert and the city, and I need someone who can greet them, put them at their ease, and speak for me when I do not wish to speak for myself. I know it is not usual to have a woman in that position, but then, it is not usual for a woman to conduct her own business dealings either. I feel you will represent me better than a man could do."

She stood, vacating the chair Nadab had offered her, and servants scurried out of the room's quarters to stand ready to assist her. She ignored them and addressed Nadab instead. "The praise I heard was not amiss. Let your daughter come to me at the nearest hour, washed and dressed. I will send you the payment we discussed straightaway."

She smiled at Rechab as she exited the house, and spoke with her voice lowered. "Come to me as quickly as you can. There is much to be done."

Alack sat on a rock by his favourite brook and kept a close eye on his sheep as they wandered along its banks, grazing on the lush growth there, drinking from the waters, and nipping each other. Overhead the cloudless sky blazed into a scorched blue. He was grateful for the shade of the willow under which he sat.

His father had watered his sheep here, and his father before him, and his father before him. The world had turned and fortunes changed for many, yet the shepherds kept their sheep, tightened their belts when need be, and let the sun darken their skin to leather. "Let the world worry about itself," Naam had often told him. "Our world does not change."

But it *would* change—if the prophet's vision came to pass, the marching army would swarm over this very ground on its way up to Shalem and the surroundings towns and villages. This would become a valley of destruction and terror.

Kol Abaddon, the prophet had called himself. The Voice of Destruction. Alack could not remove that conversation from his mind. The prophet's words had chilled him—and yet, somehow, Flora's prying questions had done something Alack had never seen before.

They had revealed that this Voice was a man.

Flora Infortunatia, they called her. Flora the Unlucky, the Unhappy. Alack knew the stories as well as anybody; they were favourites of the townspeople. Flora Infortunatia, the governor's sister, was infamous for her origin, her beauty, her marriages, and her wealth. Her "fanaticism," as some put it, made her doubly infamous. But she was a real person too, he thought—like the prophet. The conversation in the night had revealed that also.

Had it also revealed him to himself?

"This boy sees visions," the prophet had said. "He sees my visions."

Was he then also a prophet?

His father's pronouncements that nothing ever changed had always contained a measure of satisfaction in the fact; what would Naam think if his son suddenly began to see visions and dream dreams? If he were to be driven into the wilderness and howl with anguish in the night?

And what would Rechab think?

He groaned aloud.

Oh, Rechab.

Her refusal to come into the light last night had meant something, and he had not missed it. She would not be his to look upon much longer. Things were changing; things had changed. Time and circumstance had happened to them, as she had always known they would.

He had known it too. But refused to accept it.

Perhaps going into the wilderness and becoming a half-mad seer was not such a bad fate. Better than staying here and watching Rechab married to someone else while he remained poor, helpless, and pathetic in the sheepfolds and the dirt.

It occurred to him that he could simply present his case to Nadab.

Perhaps Rechab's father would be moved by his love. How many girls married men who really loved them? Who would care for them? And Alack would do well for himself, as shepherds went. He was hardworking and dedicated.

Unless of course the visions kept recurring and drove him out of his mind.

But he set that possibility aside. He could not go to Nadab the Trader and present himself as a-good-option-barring-pending-insanity.

He could wash his face and dress in his finest clothes and go to Nadab and try to posture his way into acceptance. Barring that, he could beg.

He had almost convinced himself that this was a good idea—better than doing nothing—when he became aware of someone standing on the other side of the brook. The sheep had not reacted to the presence, and Alack had been so deep in thought that he hadn't noticed him.

He lifted his eyes now and saw him clearly:

It was the prophet.

The man was simply standing there, looking at him. His skin was dark and cracked with the sun; he did not seem to notice the rays beating down on him. He made no move toward the shade of the tree. His eyes burned. Burned right into Alack.

He spoke. "Come with me. I want to show you something."

Alack reached for his shepherd's crook, but he tightened his fingers around it without lifting it off the ground. "I cannot come. My sheep . . ."

"The angels will tend your sheep. Answer my summons, boy."

Alack looked from side to side, as though trying to see the angels. Or any sign of Naam, who would not be pleased to find his boy abandoning his post in the middle of the day.

"Come," the prophet said again, and he turned and began to walk away.

Alack scrambed to his feet and splashed through the brook after him.

The prophet headed down the slope of the mountain into the desert valley below. Crags of rock marked the way, casting some shade in which twisted juniper trees and other scrub grew. Alack scurried to catch up with him, but the prophet's long legs kept his stride just out of Alack's ability to match. He found himself constantly falling behind and having to jog to catch up again.

The prophet had appeared at midday, and when he at last ceased walking, the sun was beginning to set.

Alack, sweating and dogged with exhaustion and thirst, came to a halt behind him and leaned on his shepherd's crook. "What is it," he gasped, "that you wish to show me?"

They stood atop a mountain. Its slopes were barren rock. From here Alack could look back and see the holy mountain and Shalem, the Holy City, glowing fiery in the setting light. Too, he could look around and see the valleys of the wilderness stretching out on every side. Beyond these mountains were other cities of the Holy People, and beyond them other kingdoms, nations, and empires. To the west, the Great Sea where the family of Aurelius Florus Laurentinus had come from glittered just in sight. He caught his breath.

"I did not know the Great Sea was visible from here."

"Only because the air is so clear. It is leagues off."

Alack turned and looked across the wilderness to the north of the Holy City. He could make out the greener hills of the Lake Country with its two great lakes—one living and one dead. And there, glittering on the slope of the Holy Mountain, Bethabara—above other towns and villages of the slopes.

"What did you want to show me?" he asked again, his eyes still fixed on the panorama before him.

"The Sacred Land," the prophet said.

"But I have seen it before. I have lived my whole life in the Sacred Land." Alack turned, quizzical. The prophet had seated himself on a stone and sat with his arms folded.

"You have never been here before," the prophet said.

"No."

"Then you have only seen the parts of the land. Never the whole.

When you are close to something, you are blind to its true nature. Only when you go higher can you truly see."

It sounded like one of Flora's wise sayings. Alack pondered it and knew it to be true. From this height, in the thin, clear desert air, he could see more than he had ever dreamed of the land he had always called home. Its scope, its changing landscapes, even its relative smallness.

The prophet leaned back against his rock and closed his eyes. For a moment Alack thought he was going to sleep.

Then he said, "Wait, and you will see still more."

Alack found himself another rock and sat, balancing his crook across his knees as he duly waited. His throat burned with thirst. He took out a goatskin and gave himself a small drink of water—he had been carefully rationing it all day, not knowing how long the prophet would walk. He was glad that he had done so; if he had simply given in to his thirst, he would have run out long ago.

The prophet did not carry a skin, and Alack had not seen him stop to drink or eat even once. He did not know how he had not fainted in the desert heat. But admittedly, there was much about the prophet he did not know.

The warm water calmed his parched throat and tongue a little, though it could not answer the gnawing in his stomach.

The wait, which he had expected to take minutes, stretched into hours.

The sun sank farther below the western horizon, glittering off the far distant sea, casting light and shadows and colours across the wilderness and the Holy City, making the desert dance. Alack watched in fascination at the beauty of it.

At last the temple roof blazed with one last reflective fire, and then its light winked out. Shadows had fallen.

RACHEL STARR THOMSON

Above, the stars were appearing.

Great stars in their celestial story. Many that Alack knew, and many more that he did not—more could be seen from this vantage point also.

The prophet spoke for the first time in two hours; he had not stirred since his last words.

"From a high place, not only does the world become clearer, but so do the heavenlies. You find yourself between them, listening to what one says about the other."

Alack's response to the stars the other night, the feeling that they watched him with a wisdom and accusation he found frightening, struck him again now. But there was more than that. Now he looked on them with awe.

"From here, I can understand why many in the Holy City worship the stars."

The prophet's face was a darkness. "Yes," was all he said.

He moved from his place, came to Alack's side and laid an arm across the boy's shoulders. He pointed to the sky. "Do you see that woman?" he asked.

Alack did. She was one of the marvels of the sky—the constellation Isha, a woman running.

"She is the Beloved, the Holy City," said Kol Abaddon. "Now look. And see what approaches her."

Alack followed the prophet's pointing finger to the west, and his breath caught in his throat.

"The Dragon," he said.

"He will soon overtake her and devour her whole. But look—she does not resist him. She is not running from him, but to him—rushing to him as to a lover's arms. She flings herself to Abaddon. Destruction."

The prophet lowered his finger and stepped back, turning his head to regard Alack carefully. "This too is a part of our vision."

"But . . . I don't understand. How can—"

"When you are down in the valley, you can see only the valley. From the mountain slope, you see only what is before you and beside you. You must come to a high vantage point if you are to know more. To see more, to understand more. Only in the heights will the stars speak to you." The moonlight shone in the prophet's eyes. "This is the invitation given to you, Alack son of Naam the shepherd. Every vision is only a call to come up higher, to learn what there is to be learned. What you saw is not to be lightly esteemed. The Great God himself is calling you up. Whether you will answer the call is your decision."

"What happens . . . if I do?"

"Then you will see wonders."

"But it will change everything. My whole life. I will become . . . like you."

The prophet bowed his head. "Yes."

"But Rechab . . . and my father . . ."

"A call to come up higher is a call to leave all else behind."

Alack stared at the ground. The prophet reached out and tipped his head up, pointing his eyes back to the stars. To Isha, the Beloved, and the Dragon prepared to devour her.

"It is not only for your own sake that the Great God calls. One who sees must also become one who speaks, so that others may hear the warning and choose to act. Or not."

Alack's heart beat faster as he contemplated the stars and the vision, and the prophet's many terrible warnings. "But can we change it? How can men change the courses of the stars?"

The prophet did not answer that. His eyes had strayed away from Alack, he seemed no longer to be listening. Alack followed his gaze again and found it resting this time upon the Holy Mountain and the city that was still visible there, marked by the lights that would burn all night.

Shalem, the heart of their people. The Chosen City of the Great God.

In an instant he saw the lights winked out. A shadow, huge and ominous and blacker than night, lay over the mountain.

Then it was gone. He blinked.

"Did you see that?" he asked.

"Whatever you saw, it was a vision. Yours. An invitation. Do you want to know more? Then you must go higher. If you refuse the visions, you may go back to your sheep and die with everyone else, knowing that you could have warned them and did not."

For a moment, Alack thought he understood a little of the wild man's anguish.

"I do not know," he said, "what I will do."

CHAPTER 4

A lack trudged home in the early hours of the morning. Before his leavetaking the prophet had produced strips of dried wild goat from a cleft in the rock, along with several skins of sour wine, and they had eaten their fill together. All the way back to the brook and his flocks, Alack pondered the prophet's words, the doom in the sky, and the vision of a shadow over the Holy City.

The gentle lowing of his sheep alerted him when he was nearly there, and one of his dogs came to greet him, curious and wagging its tail. A cursory inspection satisfied him that no harm had come to his sheep; they were all there, and all seemed peaceful and quiet. He only hoped Naam had not found reason to come and check on him during the day; his absence would not be easily explained.

What would his father say, if he knew what Alack was contemplating?

Abandon his sheep, abandon the service of his father, and go out into the wilderness to seek more visions. That was the choice offered to him. The path trodden by prophets and seers throughout the ages. In truth, in olden days one gifted by visions would have gone to seek direction in the Holy City itself, sacrificing in the temple and seeking counsel of the priests. But by all accounts the temple was not the place it had once been. Flora had said she refused to go into the city. Rechab was terrified of it.

He wondered if the darkness both women felt there was the same as the shadow he had seen briefly from the desert mountain.

His near plan of the day before taunted him. He had been on the verge of throwing himself headlong into seeking after Rechab's hand, a doomed mission perhaps, but one that seemed right. Else her chances of ending up at the mercy of that shadow seemed great. If he went out and became a wandering madman like the prophet, what would become of Rechab?

And if he did not, if he did not learn messages to speak from the Great God, what would become of everyone?

"But it will do no good!" he burst out, startling his dog. He fixed his eyes on the animal and addressed it. "The people do not listen. When the prophet comes to them, they listen to Aurelius instead. And even if they did. What if all the people in Bethabara believed the prophet. What good would it do? The shadow would still lie over the Holy City."

But his heart told him that he would find no answers to his questions unless he answered the call of the Great God and did as Kol Abaddon had told him to do—sought high places from which to see and hear and understand.

But the cost!

It would cost him Rechab—whatever slight chance he might have with Nadab would disappear forever.

It would cost him his life as he knew it.

And it would cost him the comforting perspective with which he lived. That of the world immediately around him, without thought of dragons in the sky and shadows and armies.

He laughed.

What did any of that matter? If he held on to his little world and found himself thrust through with a sword or an arrow, dying on the slopes of the Holy Mountain as the terrible army of the Great God marched through, he would lose everything anyway.

He sat down and fondled his dog's soft ears. "It is not much of a choice at all," he said. "The world is not easy for a man, my friend. Not even for a shepherd like me. There are too many questions with no good answers."

Even as he said the words, he knew his mind was made up.

As he had said: there was no real choice.

⎯⎯•◆•⎯⎯

Flora had sent letters to the Holy City ahead of her journey, so the merchants with whom she had come to trade knew of her arrival and began to attend on her within two days. Rechab, dressed in her finest, met them at the door of Flora's apartments with confidence and ease. With every passing hour, her confidence grew. And with it, her happiness. However temporarily, Flora had rescued her from her daily walk with impending doom and given her the gift of friendship and a window into a way that life could be very different.

Rechab had not expected the sheer numbers of men who would come; they came until they were lined up in waiting, and their retinues had to be attended and their camels and asses watered and themselves fed and entertained. Aurelius's courtyard was full, and the streets outside his house were lined with tents and picketed camels. Flora held court over the whole assembly, sparkling and shining and intimidating, driving hard bargains and striking home her wit and intelligence.

When she held private audience with one or another of the merchants, Rechab oversaw the entertaining of all the others; when Flora made herself more public, Rechab stayed by her side. Those moments were her favourite: she was as charmed by the governor's infamous sister as anyone else, and joyed in the way that Flora looked at her not as a servant but as a comrade.

The whole experience was heady. By evening of the second day, Rechab felt her exhaustion in every bone of her body and in the growing fuzz of her mind, but one thought had grown larger and more central to her every moment:

Perhaps Flora needed such help all the time.

Perhaps she would pay Nadab the Trader for Rechab's help as a servant, and Nadab would accept that price instead of the bridewealth he looked for. And then Rechab would go away with Flora into the desert and serve her, and together they would stay far away from the Holy City. Perhaps Alack could follow them. Perhaps . . .

"Rechab," Flora said. "Attend on me, please."

It was deep evening; the sun had nearly set, and most of the merchants had left the town to go to their encampments elsewhere. A few still loitered, but these Aurelius's servants were presently attending. Rechab stood in the anteroom of Flora's main apartment. She nodded and hastily answered the summons.

Flora closed the door behind her and all but collapsed into a chair. She had been sitting there as a queen all day; now she was simply and clearly an exhausted woman. Rechab set to work instantly, pouring water in a basin to wash her mistress's face and hands. Flora waved the basin away.

"No," she said, "Just come, and sit where I can see you. I want to know your opinion of some of the men today—whether they are cheating me or not."

Rechab was surprised but pleased by the request. She seated herself on a cushion on the floor and answered Flora's questions with her own honest impressions. She had quickly learned that most of Flora's wealth came from two mines in the mountains to the south, left to her by her late husband. She mined iron and copper and gems, and she did so with wisdom and a certain ruthlessness that had kept her in business for years. Both qualities were on display now. Flora listened carefully to Rechab's opinions, and the girl once more experienced a thrill at having been taken into her confidence.

When Flora seemed finished with her questions, Rechab ventured, "Will you return to your mines when these meetings are finished?"

Flora, her head resting in her hand, looked up at Rechab with surprise. "To my mines? Oh, heavens, no. I visit there only once every three years, perhaps. My home is in the desert—to the east."

Gathering up her courage, Rechab asked, "And there—do you conduct much business there?"

Flora dropped her hand. "Indeed, no. You have gathered the wrong impression of my life. All this—this wealth and these clothes and this bartering—I drop it all when I go home. There is a community in the desert of pilgrims—seekers and worshippers of the Great God. That is my home. When I am there, I am nothing. Nothing but a pilgrim. As it should be."

Rechab's heart dropped. Flora could have no need for her services, then. The hope that this life could somehow continue was gone.

"My mother," Flora said unexpectedly, "worshipped a god that was like a snake or a frog—it stood on two legs and was covered with scales, and it had two faces with a dragon's mouth and teeth in one and a man's face in the other. It is a god of the mountain people, called Kimash. She sacrificed to it in a shrine behind our home. Once, as a child, I crept into the shrine and saw the idol of Kimash standing there. The sight terrified me; for weeks, I battled with nightmares. I was convinced that Kimash wished to kill me upon its altar. I thought my mother would do it—that she would sacrifice me to the appetite of that abomination."

"But she did not," Rechab said.

"She did not. But my terror never left me. That is why, when I came to live on the Holy Mountain with my father and his family, I began to seek the Great God, who does not devour children."

She paused. "I have seen a shrine to Kimash in the Holy City, outside the gates of the temple. I wonder if it terrifies the children of the People as it does the children of the hills."

Flora stood and laid a hand on Rechab's shoulder. "I thank you for your good service today. And I urge you to do as I have done: no matter the wealth that may present itself to you in this world, nor the gods and shadows that may terrify you, run to the shelter of the Great God and seek out the shadow of his wings. Your heart is already calling you in that direction. Answer that call—follow your heart's urgings."

But I cannot, Rechab wanted to say. My heart wishes a marriage that will never be allowed. It wants distance from the Holy City, but my path must take me into its heart. My heart wants to stay and serve you, but you will not take servants.

She spoke none of that. Only lowered her eyes and nodded.

"Look at me," Flora said.

Rechab lifted her eyes and forced herself to lock gazes with the older woman, despite the protest she felt.

"It may cost you to run to the Great God," Flora said. "But no cost is too high."

Rechab blinked away tears she had not known were gathering in her eyes.

"Come back to me tomorrow," Flora said. "The merchants will continue to come for a fortnight. I wish you to attend upon me all that time. I have paid your father well to leave you with me while he goes to the Holy City in that time."

"I thank you," Rechab stuttered.

Flora looked curiously at her. "There is something you wanted to say. Something bothering you."

"I hoped . . ." Rechab cut herself off.

"Say it. You have no reason to fear me. It is as I told Kol Abaddon: I am nothing."

You are not nothing, Rechab responded silently, but in words she said, "I had hoped you might need a servant for a longer term. That . . ."

". . . that I might save you from this life?" Flora looked troubled. "If you were a slave, I would buy you and set you free. But you are a wealthy man's daughter; I do not think there is anything I can do. I cannot be your salvation, Rechab, only your friend." She smiled gently. "But I will be your friend. I promise you that."

Nadab the Trader stood in his courtyard and oversaw the preparations for his journey to the Holy City. Servants piled merchandise and foodstuffs and travel supplies in the midst of the courtyard where he could approve them; he sent some scuttling off for more while he sent others to put some things back. He expected the journey to be two weeks in duration.

The preparations were inefficient because of Rechab's absence; she had become an expert manager, and he felt the lack of her keenly. Ah well, he told himself, best get used to that. She would not be within his household much longer, even if Flora Infortunatia had not requested her help on the other side of the town.

In fact, it would be this trip that most likely decided Rechab's fate. He had planned to take her along, a fact which he presented quite forcefully to Flora until she offered him enough to make up for his disappointment, but upon reflection, he felt it was better this way. Rechab did not like the Holy City, and were she to get wind of his arrangements, he suspected she would not like them either. Best that she not have opportunity to present herself in a bad light. The man in question had seen her enough times to be convinced of her beauty and usefulness, and he badly wanted partnership with Nadab besides. The dowry he should receive for her would make her one of his best investments—certainly better than any ream of cloth or flock of sheep he had bartered. To say nothing of the powerful connections this man represented.

"My lord," one of his servants murmured, "there is a shepherd here to see you."

"What?" he bellowed. "Speak up."

"There is a shepherd here to see you. One of your suppliers."

"Now?" Nadab asked, annoyed. "I am busy. Tell the fellow to come back later."

"I did tell him, sir, but he is most insistent that he must see you now."

"Who is it? Abia? That old goat Naam?"

"A boy, sir. Naam's son."

Nadab tried but could not remember the boy's name—though he knew his face well enough. The lad was the same scrapper who had attached himself to Rechab when they were children; if he was not mistaken, she had some fondness for him. He cursed at the interruption, but curiosity got the better of him.

"Show him in to my receiving room. Tell me, man—from the look on his face, is this a matter of sheep?"

The servant raised his eyebrows. "I could not say, sir. It seems urgent."

Nodding, Nadab shouted out a few last orders and then retreated to the small room where he was wont to receive his suppliers and other business matters. He took his seat on a low chair and waited a few minutes before the boy appeared, sunburnt and dirty and nervous. At least, Nadab noted, the lad had made some effort to wash his face and don clean clothes—not that that negated the smell of sheep, a reek which he was convinced would never come out of any herdsman no matter how many times he dunked himself.

"Well, state your business," Nadab snapped. Curious as he was to know the boy's reasons for coming here, he saw no reason to soften the lad with undue kindness.

"I wish to speak with you about . . . about your daughter, sir."

"My daughter? What is your name?"

"Alack," the boy said, bewildered by the sudden change of question. "Alack, son of Naam."

"Yes, I know your father. Old and gnarled as a tree, but just as faithful. He is a good shepherd. If I recall correctly, you have thus far followed in his footsteps. Keep it up."

The boy seemed both encouraged and dismayed by this. He drew himself up a little taller and said, "Thank you. But I wish to speak to you about Rechab."

Nadab laughed. "Don't tell me you wish to marry her."

The boy flushed red beneath his darkened skin. "I—"

"Of course you do, any boy would. She is the most beautiful girl in this town, barring the interloper she's temporarily working for. But it's out of the question. I raised my daughter to marry a man of class and to bring in a great sum of dowry money, and you have no class, and no money. Am I not correct?"

Impressively, the boy was still on his feet and had not burst into tears. Nadab had to give him some credit, even if he was stammering for words. At last he got out, "It is as you say, sir. You know my position better than most. But it is not for me that I am here."

Now Nadab was truly surprised. He leaned forward. "Do tell."

"I . . ." The boy seemed to let down his guard deliberately. His manner became a little more relaxed, more honest. "I have always loved Rechab. If I could, I would marry her. But I know I cannot. That you will not allow it. And that I . . . I cannot take a wife. For other reasons. But I've come to ask you a favour on Rechab's behalf, because she is my friend, and I do not think she will speak for herself. Sir."

Nadab sat back and raised his eyebrows. "Go on."

"The Holy City is a terrible place," the boy blurted. "Rechab is terrified of it. I pray that you will not marry her to any man in that city. I ask you to promise me that."

Nadab could not have been more surprised, and admiration for the plucky son of a beggar swelled in his chest. "I am almost moved to do so, simply for your nerve," he said. "But I owe you no promises, and I will not do as you say. I have my own plans, boy, and I fear one uncalled meeting with you will not change them. Great things are underway for my Rechab. You will not prevent them."

Now the boy's voice shook, and his hands along with them. "But sir, I have seen—there is a terrible darkness over the Holy City. A shadow. And the stars portend something awful. Destruction is coming."

"Stars? Shadows? Next you will tell me the army of the Great God is going to come marching out of the west, swarming like locusts into the city."

"But they will, sir. As the prophet has said. I would that you and your daughter would leave this land. Surely there are profits to be had elsewhere . . ."

"You don't tell me my business!" Nadab roared. "Especially not with this nonsense! What do you mean, 'you have seen'? Are you a prophet too?"

The boy met his eyes. "Yes. Or I will become one. I am telling you what I saw, and only what I saw. Terrible destruction is coming."

"Then why are *you* staying here?" Nadab demanded.

The boy's voice shook again, but his gaze did not waver. "Because someone must be a voice. Maybe it is not too late."

Nadab stood and paced a few steps, regarding the boy with a sideward glance. He was strangely moved.

"Here now, boy," he said. "I make you an offer: you must promise to stay away from Rechab and make no interference concerning her. If you will make me that promise, I will raise you up from the sheepfold. I will take you with me to the Holy City—after you have taken about twenty baths—and teach you my trade, and you will serve close to my left hand. One day perhaps you will have the money to pay a good bride price for another. And you may leave this talk of destruction and prophecy behind you."

For a split second Nadab saw that the boy was considering it. But then he was shaking his shaggy head, loosing grains of sand that fell upon the floor.

"You are generous. But I cannot."

"Nor can I accept your warnings or your requests. You do understand that?"

"I understand."

"I am a man of the world. I do not know what may or may not be coming upon us. I do know what price my Rechab will bring and how she will be cared for, and I know what dealing with the Holy City has done for my life and my table from thirty years past until today. You would do well to consider these things. You are dismissed."

With an unhappy nod, the boy turned to go.

CHAPTER 5

Flora Laurentii followed her first day of business by setting up a sanctuary within Aurelius's rooms, a tiny space five feet by five feet where she could resort to pray. And resort she did, three times a day no matter what else was going on, while Rechab calmly adjured Flora's visitors to wait. Aurelius chafed at this, as he did the constant flow of guests and merchantmen, though the latter was a thorn in his side not because it was any sign of piety, but because in her way, Flora was making herself look more important than he. When had Aurelius the Governor ever had such an influx of guests seeking his presence or his wealth?

"A circus," he muttered to Marah on the third day, while camels and servants milled about his courtyard and still others in the street outside; "a zoo."

Marah pulled a grape from the cluster she was eating and said nothing as she sucked it.

"And she does not even attend upon them as she should. Do you know where she is right now? She is praying in that closet of hers."

Marah smiled. "That only bothers you because you would not dare to keep such a congregation of important men waiting, and Flora will. She is making you jealous, Husband, and that makes you look small."

Aurelius grimaced. His breakfast, grapes and raisins and fish laid out before him, entirely failed to entice him.

"When you look small you are unattractive, even to me," Marah continued. "And you respond foolishly. This is a great opportunity, Aurelius. These merchantmen may not all be noble, but their wealth is great, and they come from many nations. And they are all in *your* house. They are not loyal to Flora; they attend upon her only for her money. So there is no reason you may not court their favour as well. Leave your smallness behind and make something of this."

"But she has bypassed me," Aurelius said, "and set the child of Nadab the Trader in the place that I should occupy."

"Nonsense; it would make you ridiculous to do what the girl is doing. Invite the men into meetings of your own. Feast them, wine them. Learn their news and their ways. Get their secrets out of them, and pretend to give them some of yours. You are a politician, Aurelius. Politicize. Start now, while they are all waiting for her to cease her prayers."

As Marah spoke, a glimmer of hope dawned in Aurelius's mind. It was true: this was a great opportunity. He had been too busy sulking to notice it, as though he were still a boy and Flora still the little sister who stole his father's attention during the summer and who always whined and cried and got him into trouble.

Astonishing how little had changed, really.

But why not use her wealth and success to bolster his own career? Why not, indeed? More and more, the business of the Holy City was to deal with the nations—nations from which these men came, and in which they had no little influence or wealth. Of course he should do all he could to learn who they were, to make alliances where he could, perhaps even to identify enemies.

One never knew when friends would prove useful.

Aurelius strode into the courtyard a new man. A trader had just arrived, dressed in the pale robes of the Southern Plains, the once great region to the south. Many of the Hill People were among his slaves, which caused Aurelius to smirk; these were his sister's kin, many of them wearing the amulets and symbols of their horrid gods around their necks. At least his father's people worshipped gods that looked and acted like men. The half-breed fish and serpents and dragons of the hills debased those who worshipped them. The slaves made way for him quickly, bowing and scraping as he approached their master with open arms and a loud greeting.

This day would be busier, and more fruitful, than he had thought.

———— ◆ ————

As the governor's newfound hospitality suddenly eased the burden on Rechab, she found herself gripped with fear. Would Flora dismiss her early? Aurelius seemed bent on entertaining all of these guests while Flora prayed or dealt with only a few of them; surely Rechab's job was superfluous.

Flora herself dismissed that fear quickly, and without Rechab needing to voice it. "My brother would cheat me royally if he could get away with it," she said with a wink. "I need you here to keep an eye and an ear out. Besides, Aurelius is just entertaining them; I still need a go-between to speak for me and an aide to manage my affairs. Fear not, my girl, you are stuck with me for the full fortnight of your hire. Besides, I would hate to try to get money back from your father."

So it was that when Nadab the Trader left Bethabara for the Holy

City, Rechab stood in the street and waved him away, every step he took lightening her spirits. She did not have to go. This time at least, she was safe here.

She scanned the street for any sign of Alack. He had not come to see her since she began working for Flora two days ago—no surprise, really. But he would learn that she was still here, and he would come.

Despite knowing that they could have no future, Rechab looked forward to that.

So her heart sank a little when, scanning the crowds that had gathered to gawk at Nadab's leavetaking, she could see no sign of the young shepherd.

He is in the fields, she told herself. He has duties too, you know. He will come when he can.

Alack had never failed to come to her. Somehow he always knew where she was and how to find her. She winced as she thought back to their last conversation—to her own refusal to encourage him. But how could she? What hope was there?

She strongly suspected her father had already sold her to someone, and she would go away and never see Alack again. A wash of sudden tears blurred her vision and she turned away, wishing she could blink away the pain in her chest as easily as she could clear her eyes. Maybe she had not guarded her heart against this as thoroughly as she thought she had.

Maybe, in the end, there was no real way to guard against heartbreak.

Run to the Great God, Flora had told her. It may cost you everything. But you must do it.

She wondered what Flora knew about cost, and then rebuked herself. Flora's life might be a joke to everyone else, but it could not have been a joke to live through, or to be known to everyone as the Unlucky. She remembered Flora's account of the hill god Kimash and shivered.

It was true that there was a shrine to Kimash outside the temple. Rechab had once glimpsed past the curtain to the eerily lit statue standing there—she had torn her eyes away as quickly as possible and looked instead to the high walls and glimmering golden roof of the temple of the Great God.

"Ugh," she said aloud as she moved her feet back to the house of Aurelius and her current employment. Talking to herself helped take her mind away from the images that wanted to flood it. "Why must you think of the one place you don't want to be? You are here now. Just *be* here."

For a fortnight at least, she was free.

A sudden commotion in the street up ahead distracted her from her chosen path; at first she meant to ignore it, but the noise and the urgency grew, and she found herself running to see what was happening. She was not the only one. Other townspeople poured down the narrow streets toward the broad road where someone was shouting incoherent but ear-splitting things.

The scene in the road was the last thing she expected to encounter.

One of Flora's visitors had camped at the roadside with his retinue—the great man from the Southern Plains. Tents and camels and chests of goods lined the road for yards. But none of that was the focus now. One of the man's slaves, a small, dark fellow from the Hill People, was crouched in the midst of the road, wailing eerily. He clutched an amulet in one hand and a knife in the other, and he was stripped nearly naked. His eyes burned with an expression that was not human; for a moment Rechab caught his eye, and she gasped and looked away in fear.

Eight of the trader's men were circling around the slave, some with swords in hand and two holding a net as though they would snare the fellow. They too were shouting, but the words were all in the Hill People tongue, and Rechab did not know them. The slave menaced them with his knife, and though he was much smaller and more poorly armed than they, they seemed afraid.

"What is happening?" she asked an older woman who was lingering beside a wall.

"The slave is daemonized," the woman said. "See; the men are trying to subdue him, but they fear the power of the hill gods."

Only once before had Rechab seen anyone in this condition—it had been one of the People, a villager from a town near Bethabara. But that man had not been dangerous. When the daemon had taken him, he was thrown down in frothing, helpless fits. Everyone had pitied him.

Suddenly the slave's dark finger was pointed directly at Rechab.

The woman beside her gasped and stepped away, and all eyes followed the line to her. She heard the murmuring and questions but could not tear her eyes away from the man.

"You!" he said, cackling. "You belong to us! Sold, sold, sold—to us!"

Rechab's heart plummeted.

But then another voice rang over the road, and Flora Laurentii Infortunatia stepped out of the confines of a narrow street and into the ring formed by the trader's men. They leaped at her, as though to bodily pull her away, but she held up a hand and stayed them. Her eyes were fixed on the slave.

"It is not true!" she said. "I bind your words and deny them in the name of the Great God. What authority do you have over this child?"

"She is sold to us," the slave hissed, his eyes darting from Flora to Rechab. The armed men, he ignored entirely. Where they had not seemed to cow him in the least, Flora clearly made him nervous.

"Be gone, vermin!" Flora commanded, pointing her finger directly at the man. "By the power of the Great God, get thee out!"

The slave let out a scream that rent the air, and he seemed to crumple where he stood—falling to his knees and then curling inward until he lay in the dust as a dead man. At the same time, Flora fainted, and no one was close enough to prevent her fall.

———◆———

Aurelius's men arrived just in time to cart Flora back to the governor's house, with Rechab following anxiously behind. She had recovered consciousness before they reached the house, and although everyone insisted that she lie down in one of the cooler apartments and take a drink before she would be allowed to rise, she was clearly unhappy about complying. She called for Rechab as soon as she could form words, and the girl soon found herself alone with Flora, trying to minister a cup of cold water but being soundly denied.

"Put it aside," Flora insisted, waving the cup away. She could not quite lift her head but had lost nothing of her determination. "You heard what he said."

"You said it wasn't true," Rechab said.

"I denied his authority and bound his words. And they shall not be true. They will not have you. But I do not doubt they think they have some claim, and that will be bad news for you, Rechab. You cannot stay here."

Panic tried to rise in Rechab's heart, but she shoved it back down. Her hands were shaking—whether from Flora's words or from the whole traumatic scene, she did not know. "But what am I to do? Where can I go?"

"Run to the Great God."

"You told me that," Rechab said, blinking tears away, "but it does not help me. Where does the Great God dwell? In the Holy City, in Shalem, in the temple. But even you will not go there. He is not there, and something dark has taken his place. You know this. So how can I run to him? To a god who is invisible and who has no home on this earth?"

Flora considered the words for all of three seconds and said, "You will come with me."

Surprise and hope alike flickered, though not strong enough to beat back the waves of fear and protest that were throbbing through her now. "But you said you cannot use me where you live. And you did not think my father would sell you my services."

"I can't, and he will not, especially not if he has sold you to the gods somehow. They will not allow him to break their grip, and he is not a good man, so he will not able to do it of himself." She looked a bit apologetically at Rechab, but Rechab waved it away. The words were true enough.

Flora continued, "It does not matter, I will not try to buy your services. You must run away. But I will allow you to hide with me."

"I can't."

"You have to."

"He'll follow me. They'll guess where I've gone."

"What if they do? You have no other choice, Rechab." Flora swung her legs around and sat up, wincing and touching a hand to her head. Even sitting, she looked unsteady.

"What happened back there?" Rechab asked. "This . . . what happened to you?"

"I tried to exorcise a daemon. I think I did it. I have never done it before."

"But all you did was speak. How has it made you so weak?"

"You think words are not power? You have much to learn."

Flora winced outwardly now and reached for the water Rechab had tried to give her before. "Let me drink. I need just a moment."

Rechab handed the water to her and stepped back. Somehow the encounter had made Flora strange to her—almost as strange, and as frightening, as the daemoniac.

"I wish I could speak with Alack," Rechab blurted, instantly kicking herself for saying the words aloud.

"The shepherd boy?" Flora asked, surprised.

"Yes. He is my friend."

Flora frowned. "I think he will be far from here by now."

"What—what do you mean?"

Flora's voice grew gentler. "Kol Abaddon means to disciple the boy, I am sure. If Alack answered his call, he will be out in the wilderness—learning to hear the Great God and see his visions."

"But I need him here!" Rechab said, turning her back tightly and hugging her stomach. Everything combined was making her feel sick, and it was all she could do to keep the panic down. No, it was not fair that Alack should have gone. Surely he wouldn't go—wouldn't abandon her here! But he had thought she was going to the Holy City with her father. Maybe he didn't know. Maybe . . .

"You must not look to a man to save you," Flora said. "You must do as I say and run to the Great God. Take my offer: we will leave here tomorrow and go back to the desert, to Essea—the community where I live. My teachers can show you more about the Great God and teach you to worship him."

"I don't know if I want to worship him," Rechab said. "If he is so weak that idols can fill his temple and so cold that he would take Alack away from me now."

Flora was silent. Rechab waited a painfully long time and then turned. Flora was simply watching her, with an expression that was both thoughtful and sympathetic. Rechab had expected condemnation, so the expression caught her off balance and softened her a little—just enough to break the grip of panic and bitterness.

"I am sorry. I am speaking out of fear."

"I know."

"Why would the hill gods want anything to do with me?"

"I don't know. I only know their nature is to devour. I ran from them once too—to the Great God. And he accepted me. Do the same, Rechab."

For a long moment they looked into each other's eyes, Rechab's deep brown and Flora's startling green.

"I will go," Rechab said.

CHAPTER 6

A lack's journey had taken him two days into the wilderness, and still no sign of the prophet.

With every step, he replayed the final scenes in his mind. Farewell to the sheep. Farewell to his father, who was not angry—who instead was brokenhearted, and so broke Alack's heart. Farewell to life as he knew it. He remembered also the ill-fated conversation with Nadab, and the thought of Rechab's face.

The one farewell he had not said.

The one he *could* not say.

He knew she had not left Bethabara with his father—that Flora Laurentii had hired her to manage her business affairs. He wanted to go and tell her what he was doing, but he could not.

Because for all that Rechab pretended she had kept her heart safe from him, for all that she treated him like they were only friends, he knew that she would not want him to go. And if she asked him to stay, he might do the unthinkable.

He might deny the call of the Great God and remain a shepherd in Bethabara.

Knowledge that he had done the right thing did little to ease the pain in his heart as he took step after sun-weary step, his eyes sweeping the rocky, barren land for some sign of the man he wished to find.

He would not have left when he did—he would have waited for Kol Abaddon to come to the town again. But something had happened. He had heard a voice. Only brief—but undeniable. Telling him to go out into the desert and he would find the prophet there.

If Alack was going to become a prophet himself, he could not start by disobeying the voice of the Great God when he was fairly certain he had heard it.

Of course, some confirmation of that would be nice too. Like actually finding the prophet out here like he had expected to.

He had not begun his wandering two days ago with any particular strategy. Assured that he would find Kol Abaddon in the wilderness, he'd just started walking and assumed he would find him quickly and be redirected from there. But a morning's walk, a hot afternoon's rest, and an evening's walk again had not revealed the prophet's current hideaway, and so on the second day Alack employed a little more sense and veered east toward a series of low valleys where he and his father often pastured their sheep and where there were water and caves and places for madmen to hide.

The thought of madmen made him a little nervous. It was not unheard-of that robbers would hide here, or men who were genuinely mad or possessed by daemons. Small bands of displaced Hill People also lurked here, most of them up to little good. He and his father had experienced small run-ins before, but then they had always had the dogs, and each other, and often the company or at least the assurance of other shepherds nearby. Now he was alone.

Evening's onset was turning the desert blue, and Alack began seeking out the sides of the valleys for a small cave where he could shelter

RACHEL STARR THOMSON

for the night. Somewhere not far away a jackal barked and laughed. The sandy ground before him was already beginning to cool.

A dark blot on the valley side drew his attention; he had been here before. The climb was not arduous, but a ledge just beneath the cave itself required scrambling over and provided a little more protection from anything coming up from below. Four-legged assailants, in any case, were unlikely to bother with it.

The cave was warm and dry, shallow but sheltered, and Alack settled back into its farthest corner after checking for snakes with his staff. He set his staff across his knees and closed his eyes for a few moments, letting his body calm and settle.

When he opened his eyes again, the stars were beginning to come out.

On the horizon he could see them rising—and there they were, the stars Kol Abaddon had shown him: the Dragon and Isha, the Beloved. It seemed to him that they had moved closer together, and Alack felt a deep dread as he gazed at them. That was his world up there in the sky—the Holy People, the Beloved City, the Chosen of the Great God, rushing toward a predator far worse than any jackal or lion or mountain marauder could ever be. But why?

The sight too much for him, he closed his eyes again—

And saw the army.

They were thousands, tens of thousands, strong. They swarmed over the wilderness, over the desert and the valleys—no, not swarmed, but marched, side by side, one against another, their shields locked like a dragon's great scaled armour twisting across the face of the earth. The sound of their feet marching shook the ground and filled the sky and vibrated through Alack's bones until his teeth chattered, and they came so close he could see their faces and their eyes—

He blinked and rocked backwards, hitting his head on the cave wall. "Ow!" he exclaimed, and touched his head gingerly—he was all right. And the vision was over.

But he had seen them so clearly, and learned something that shocked and disturbed him.

These soldiers—they looked like Aurelius.

He frowned, his head still aching, trying to recall exactly what they had looked like—he could see their eyes under their bronze helmets, many of them blue or green, their skin lighter than the People's, their noses strong. They were Aurelius's kin, certainly.

Kol Abaddon appeared directly in front of him in the cave mouth and startled him so badly that he jumped, this time smashing his head against the cave roof.

He woke up to Kol Abaddon bending over him and the stars shining in a blue sky overhead.

"Are you all right, boy?" the prophet was asking.

"Yes," he said groggily. "I hit my . . . head . . ."

"Jumped like a fool. Weren't you expecting me?"

"Well, yes, but . . ."

The prophet's strong hand grasped his and hauled him to his feet. "You're in the wilderness. It's a dangerous place. You should be more aware."

"I know that," Alack said, dusting himself off and wincing at the pain slicing through his head. "I've been out here before many times. But I—"

He stopped as the memory rushed back. "The Great God's army! They look like Aurelius!"

Kol Abaddon regarded him curiously. "Yes," he said. "They do."

"I saw them again . . . just before you appeared. That's why I didn't hear you. I was trying to remember their faces."

"You do not need to remember. They will be ever before you."

It was true. He could still see them with crystal clarity. "Why do they look like the governor?" he asked.

"Because they are the governor's people," Kol Abaddon said as though he was stating something extremely obvious. He pointed across the valley. "The people of the Westland, on the Great Sea."

"Aurelius said his people were not strong in battle."

"They were not. But things change. The Sacred Land was once protected from invaders and all other enemies. But things change. The People have invited the enemy into their heart."

"Do you mean Aurelius?" Alack asked. "Is it wrong that he is governor in Bethabara?"

Kol Abaddon snorted. "Aurelius is just Aurelius. He and his father and his father and his father before him have lived peacefully alongside the People and respected our ways. He is ambitious and sycophantic, but he is not the Dragon. And it is not his presence here that will bring the army from the west."

"Then what?"

"When was the last time you went to the Holy City?" Kol Abaddon asked.

Alack frowned. "Not since I was a boy."

"Did you know about the Calling?" the prophet asked.

"What do you mean?"

Kol Abaddon gazed away toward the Holy Mountain and Shalem at its height. "When the Great God set the People in this land, he commanded that every son of the land come to attend him once every year in Shalem. It is meant to be a great feast day."

"But . . ." Alack racked his mind for any memory of such a day—or even a mention of it. "But then why do we not go up?"

"At first we did. But then the far people, those on the borders and over them, said it was too much to come every year. The priests said they could send money with the traders instead, so they did. But those who were closer, in the Lake Country and the villages, also thought it was too much to come, and so they too sent money, and then the people on the sides of the Holy Mountain itself. Then the money ceased, and the priests did not speak up. So every year the Great God waits, but none come to attend him."

"But the priests still offer sacrifices every day," Alack said. "And the People bring them and send money."

"The People sacrifice when they want something from the Great God, but they do not ask what he wants of them. And they have filled the Holy City with idols and the gods of the nations—even the abominations of the hill countries. You saw a dark shadow over Shalem. That is the shadow. That is what the women feel when they go to the Holy City. They feel the darkness of betrayal and the enemy gods sitting where they should not be."

"And that is why the army is coming?" Alack asked.

"Because the Holy City has become an abomination," Kol Abaddon said. "Yes."

The words were not entirely a surprise. Naam and some others spoke of the idols in the Holy City as an offense. It was not uncommon to hear dissatisfaction with the priests or the sentiment that the People's worship of the Great God ought to be more fervent—and it was just as common to hear others expressing interest in the gods of the nations and dismissing any idea that the People should be loyal only to one. And yet Alack found himself wrestling with what Kol Abaddon told him. The vision of the marching army was so terrible. Kol Abaddon's warnings of the destruction it would wreak were pure horror. All of that over a few statues in the Holy City?

But it did not pay to offend a powerful god.

Alack trembled at the idea that he was entering the service of this god. And now at the idea that he himself was already an offender—one who had failed, year after year, to present himself before the Great God in the temple.

"But I did not know," he said aloud, quietly.

And he understood as he said the words. That was why he had to become a prophet. That was why he had to use his voice and speak the visions he saw and the words he heard. So that others who did not know *would* know.

So that no one else would have cause to speak the words he had just spoken.

"But can we change it?" he asked, peering through the darkness at the prophet beside him. Evening had quickly progressed into night, and it was hard to make out the wild man's features. The moonlight caught in his beard and hair like a halo. "If we tell everyone—can anything change the vision?"

"I do not know," Kol Abaddon said. "The Great God is angry. I do not know what can appease his wrath."

But the way he said it told Alack he was hiding something.

That was unexpected—so much so that Alack decided not to pursue it, for he felt he might be walking on dangerous territory.

They sat side by side in the darkness for some time, listening to the jackals and the wind. The night had been still, but now the wind chased across the desert sands and woke the shadows. On many such nights, Alack had heard the sound of the prophet himself howling into the darkness. He wanted to ask him why he howled, what tormented him so, but he feared to know. For he himself would become a prophet. There was no turning back.

Perhaps he would soon suffer such torments himself.

Perhaps, he would soon know what it meant to howl with grief or fear or madness in the night.

Why did you come here, Alack? he asked himself. What made you leave everything to do this?

There in the night, he could not answer that question. The weight of the vision. The prospect of losing Rechab. Or fascination with Kol Abaddon himself. Or perhaps it was all much deeper and much simpler than that.

Perhaps he just felt a calling, and he could not help but answer it.

After a very long time, Alack licked cracked lips and said, "I have come to follow you."

Kol Abaddon grunted.

Alack had not been entirely sure he was still awake.

"I want you to disciple me. I believe the Great God has called me to be a prophet, as you said."

Another grunt.

Alack licked his lips again. He was unsure where to go from here. How did one learn to be a prophet, exactly? Would they sit here until a vision came? Would they study the stars or wander the wilderness? Was there something one could do to cause a vision to come—like the Hill People, who would smoke certain plants or cut themselves or drive one another into a frenzy before the images of their gods?

Kol Abaddon spoke unexpectedly.

"Men are shaped by the gods they worship. The Hill People worship abominations, beasts and daemons, and so they are little better than beasts and daemons themselves. The people of the Southern Plains worship strange and distant beings that control nature, and they themselves are distant and controlled and fierce. The people of the Western Sea worship gods who are like immoral men, and they follow in the footsteps of those men—some are better than their gods, others worse. But we—we alone, the Holy People, worship an invisible god. The Great God cannot be seen. He cannot be heard with the ear. Yet he sees inside the heart of every man and hears his inmost thoughts. The Great God is above all. He creates and is not created. And so the man who worships him cannot be abased, because his god always calls him up higher, never lower."

Alack smiled as he recalled his first conversation with the prophet, when Kol Abaddon had said something similar—that every vision was a call to come up higher, and it was up to Alack to answer that call or not.

He had done it. He had left behind the sheepfold and the village and the life he had always known to sit on this valley slope with a man of God and be raised higher.

There was silence again a long time. And then Kol Abaddon said, "That is your first lesson. If you would be a prophet, look up."

Alack tried to meditate on that as Kol Abaddon again fell silent, and hours passed.

He woke when the sun was rising. He had slept on his back on the slope, rather than sheltering in a cave, and somehow had slept straight through—he sat up, disoriented, and felt his head to see if the bruise was worse than he had thought. He should not have slept so soundly. It was not safe.

A moment later he realized he was alone. He looked around wildly for the prophet but could see him nowhere. A small flock of wild goats, poised on a series of rocks on a parallel slope, watched him curiously as he jumped up and began calling out for his companion, but there was no answer, and the goats were no help.

A small tumbleweed came out of nowhere and hit him in the back of the head. He spun around and stared straight up the slope, shielding his eyes against the sun. A figure sat in a tree growing four or five yards away.

"What did I tell you?" Kol Abaddon said. "Look up."

Sheepish, Alack tried to pull himself together and began climbing the increasingly steep slope. "Did you sleep there?" he asked.

The prophet did not answer.

It was a good place to keep watch—much better than the slope where Alack had been lying out like a piece of carrion just inviting someone or something to find him. He wondered if Kol Abaddon had kept awake all night.

For that matter, taking in the man's appearance again, Alack wondered if he ever slept. Grabbing at a few roots to help himself clamber up, he drew alongside the prophet and tried to turn to gaze out across the valley. His foot slipped, and he slid a few paces down before stopping himself on a rocky outcrop.

He couldn't decide if his mentor looked amused or disgusted. At least the tumbleweed to the back of the head had indicated *some* sense of humour.

A dull ache in the back of his head let Alack know that last night's startled reactions had left their mark. He was going to have to get better at that. He suspected Kol Abaddon would be full of surprises—and he doubted he would ever grow accustomed to seeing visions.

"What are we doing today?" he asked the prophet.

He wasn't surprised when no answer came. Seeking out better footing, he scrambled up the hillside again and sat gingerly beside his mentor, noting that Kol Abaddon smelled at this close range and that something was crawling in his hair.

If he had dreamed of glory as a prophet, those dreams were succumbing to reality now. But he smirked to himself even as he thought of that. It wasn't as though his life as a shepherd was much better, in this regard at least.

He wasn't sure why he asked it, but he did. "Will Rechab be all right?"

Kol was silent for a long time, and then he stood abruptly and said, "We have all left much behind us to follow the voice of the Great God. It is better not to dwell on what is in the past."

And again, Alack felt it—he was hiding something.

He remembered the way Flora had called out Kol Abaddon's humanity, insisting that he was not inhuman and that he had needs like everyone else. That moment of insight was part of the reason Alack had decided to join the prophet. But he surely was not showing any such vulnerability now.

The prophet began his journey down the slope, walking without a staff and remarkably sure-footedly; Alack slipped and slid after him, using his staff to keep him from losing his footing completely and tumbling down the hillside. The air grew hotter as they descended into the valley, but Alack knew this region fairly well and realized that Kol Abbadon was headed for a spring. He might not sleep, and his food might be little more than locusts and the occasional strip of dried meat, but at least the prophet, like everyone else, had to drink.

Despite the prophet's admonition, Alack's thoughts drifted back to Rechab as they climbed over rocks and into sandy desert paths on their way to the spring. He hoped that she would be all right. Perhaps heaven would reward his obedience to the Great God's call by taking care of her.

He wasn't sure if things worked that way, but it felt like they should.

Of course, thinking back over Kol Abaddon's words yesterday, it was possible that the Holy People were just so deep in separation and rebellion against the Great God that he wasn't watching or thinking of them at all, other than to bring judgment on them. He imagined turning the hearts of the people with his stirring words of vision and then amassing them all together at the temple to try to call for the Great God's attention, all of them praying and fasting and sacrificing and noisemaking until the ears of heaven would turn their way.

"It is a stiff-necked people," Kol Abaddon announced. "With closed ears and shut eyes."

Alack nearly tripped, and he danced a few steps down the path as sharp-edged plants cut at his ankles. Had the prophet been reading his thoughts?

But that was all the holy man had to say.

It was all he said, in fact, for the remainder of the morning, and deep into the afternoon, and by evening, Alack was just beginning to wonder if the prophet had been struck dumb when Kol Abaddon disappeared entirely, and he was left sitting in the tangled roots of a wild olive tree by a brook somewhere far away from home.

At least this was a pleasant place to wait, but Alack felt a deep loneliness beginning to gnaw at him as he positioned his staff in hand and listened to the jackals starting up again, echoed by the calls of a nearby owl. His new mentor was very unlike his father, who was short of words but always caring and kind, and whose eyes were always on Alack. He missed Naam. And Kol Abaddon's admonition to forget the past did little to nothing to comfort his heart.

He did not know when he fell asleep, but when he awoke, the desert was silvered by a high moon and something was bleating in distress. At first he thought it was one of his lambs, but he quickly recalled where he was. A wild goat, then? Or a lost sheep?

Whatever it was, the sound tore at his heart, and he was wide awake. He picked up his staff and stood slowly, scanning his surroundings for any sign of danger. He could see but little, and yet he felt no real threat in the air—only the baaing, bleating sound of a creature in need of help.

Stumbling over obstacles too dark to see, he managed to keep relatively quiet as he moved toward the sound. He could hear the brook behind him, giving him a way to find his sleeping place again when he needed it.

He followed the sound down into a steep wadi, a narrow canyon that opened up in the valley floor and took him deeper beneath the sands. A trickle of water ran through the center of the wadi, and a few scrub trees grew along its base, forcing him to push his way past them. They scratched his arms and legs, but he ignored them, intent on finding the source of the sound.

The wadi ended where its two sides came together and met in a tight V, and there, huddled down and staring up at him with enormous eyes, was a pure white lamb. The spring flowed from the ground behind it.

Alack stood and stared at the lamb for a moment. It seemed a wonder that moonlight even reached down here, but it did, and the light illuminated the creature's form and beauty. Rarely had he ever seen such a perfect animal.

He knelt down and reached out with his hand, cooing to the creature, moving slowly forward until he laid his hand on its neck and stroked it.

"It's all right," he said. "You are lost, aren't you? It's all right; I've found you. I'll keep you safe."

The creature trembled, but he felt that his voice was calming it, so he reached out and picked it up, holding it against him until its shaking abated, talking to it all the while. His heart was full, his loneliness abated. This was the last thing he would have thought to find out here, but he was deeply glad that he had.

Suddenly he felt hope—hope for himself, for Rechab, even for the Holy People.

He talked to the lamb all the way out of the wadi, forgetting to listen for danger or even to watch for it. So it was that when he stepped out of the canyon again, he looked up and froze in fear at the sight of eyes glimmering at him from every side of the wadi's mouth.

CHAPTER 7

Marah's advice proved better than Aurelius expected in his very first conversation—with the trader from the Southern Plains, whose wisdom and knowledge were vast, both of things earthly and of things arcane. With enough wine in him, the man talked a great deal, and so it was that Aurelius first heard of the stirrings to the west and came, for the very first time, to wonder if there was something to the ravings of the mad prophet.

Not that he believed in the prophet's claims of divine inspiration, nor in his wild warnings of total destruction. But he wondered if, after all, the prophet had heard rumours that fueled his mad delusions.

The western lands on the Great Sea had been small, relatively poor, and perpetually infighting for generations. But apparently things were beginning to change, and Aurelius found himself wondering if a journey to his homeland might not be in his favour.

He looked forward to learning more from others of the merchantmen coming to his house, and so he was blindsided when Flora approached him while he was sitting at his meat and said, "I am leaving."

He blinked up at her. "Excuse me?"

"I am finished my business here; I am returning to the desert. I thank you for your hospitality. You have been most accommodating."

"But—but why?" He was sputtering. He wiped his mouth hastily and stood. "You said you would be here a fortnight. There will be others still coming to wait on you."

"I did mean to stay a fortnight, but my plans have changed." She didn't meet his eyes—a bit unusual for Flora, who was not typically cowed by anything. "I feel I am needed at home, and I want to go."

"But—"

She cut him off, meeting his eyes this time. "The traders will continue to come, as I have no way to get word to them. I imagine you will be able to make use of their company, and the town will benefit from their goods, if you are generous enough. This is no hurt to you, brother."

It would, however, be a hurt to Flora—her reputation would suffer at least a little. That fact was not lost on Aurelius, who felt calmer on his own behalf after she pointed out the obvious but now knew a rising curiosity. Why was she leaving? Unpredictable and fanatical she was, but Flora had always been a shrewd businesswoman. He had never known her to do deliberate harm to that part of her life.

But she was true to her word. She had her servants packing within minutes of her announcement, overseen by the girl Rechab. Aurelius smirked. Nadab the Trader would not be happy that he had left his daughter behind for nothing—but then, whatever Flora had paid him, she would never get it back. The merchant had not suffered overmuch, no matter how much he was likely to complain upon his return that his daughter had been left idle at home while he was in the Holy City without her.

In the courtyard, Flora's preparations created a whirlwind of activity. Shouts, brays, hustle—and all this in the midst of hosting guests.

Amon, the trader from the Southern Plains, stood in a corner of the courtyard watching the activity with a strange expression on his face. Bodyguards stood three to each side, all six of them men of the Hill People with curved swords and scarred faces. Aurelius made his way to his new friend, intent on soliciting his company at dinner, where they could talk without interruption from his sister.

Flora was leaving, and that fact was beginning to impact him as blissful freedom.

"My friend!" Aurelius called as he approached the merchant with his characteristically shaven head. "I wish to invite you to sup with me tonight. I—"

"I thank you, but no," Amon said.

Aurelius stopped in his tracks. His rebuttal came out weak, like a bleating sheep. "But I have slaughtered the best of my calves and . . ."

"I must be leaving," Amon said. His eyes were still on Flora's retinue as they worked to pack up and be gone.

"You too?" Aurelius blurted.

Amon smiled, but the smile held no warmth. Like a snake's grin. "Something must be in the wind." He turned his head and fixed his gaze on Aurelius. "I too feel a call to cross the desert."

Something in the man's tone and expression chilled Aurelius. He stammered out a response and backed away, turning to go inside. He nearly collided with Marah, who was standing just inside the door.

"What is all this?" she demanded.

"Flora is leaving," Aurelius said. "And so is Amon."

"What is it?" Marah said. "Something is troubling you."

"Flora has never left in such a rush, nor so foolishly. She says she feels a need to retun home but will explain nothing to me."

"That is not what is bothering you. There is advantage to you in her change of plans."

He marveled, as always, at how quickly his wife grasped implications that it had taken him a while to see. But that was not what held his attention now.

He lowered his voice. "I am troubled by Amon's leavetaking. He said nothing yesterday about going."

Marah peered out the door, studying Amon and his bodyguard and then watching Flora's company for a moment. She turned back to her husband. "Tell me what you fear."

"That he is planning to follow her, and means her harm."

Marah raised her eyebrows in mock surprise, but her expression said that she understood. "You have never loved Flora," she said.

"Not loving Flora was like a game in our home," Aurelius said. "And I have not entirely outgrown it. But I do not wish to see her come to harm at the hands of a mercenary trader with his eyes on her riches."

"Nor do I. So tell her what is troubling you."

"Mmm. Yes. But I can only hope she will listen."

Marah reached out and patted his cheek. "You are a better man than I take you for, sometimes."

He smiled. "And you a better woman."

In the courtyard, Rechab was busy directing procedures, trying to keep the look on her face appropriately businesslike and give away nothing of the tumult she felt. Was it exhilaration or despair that churned her insides? Was she excited to embark or terrified to flee? She could not even say.

Flora was as active as she, on the other side of the courtyard, giving orders and directing the chief among her servants. Some of her guards, hired men from the South, lingered near her and kept their eyes on the trader and his Hill People bodyguards.

Rechab trembled every time she saw them. She had not again caught sight of the slave who had fingered her in the street, but she would be glad to get away from his master and fellow servants as well. She felt a menace in their very presence that she could not explain nor dismiss.

Her duties drew her attention again, and so she only saw out the corner of her eye as the governor approached Flora and drew her, protesting, away.

Minutes later Flora had appeared at her shoulder. "Rechab, come. I need to speak with you."

They ducked into an anteroom, empty of anyone else, and Flora kept her eyes up and sharp as she spoke in a quiet voice. "Aurelius believes Amon plans to follow us."

"Why?" Rechab asked.

"He does not know, but he thinks he is up to no good. I am inclined to agree. Amon is a snake. A wealthy snake, and one it pays to know, but a serpent all the same. He will lull you one moment and swallow you the next."

"You think he would attack you?"

"He might."

"Are your guards strong enough to protect you?"

"They are strong enough at least to make it a fair fight. But it is not myself I worry for. It is you."

Rechab nearly choked. "Me?"

"It was Amon's slave who fingered you in the street. He knows that. I think you may be the treasure he wishes to steal from me."

"But what am I?" Rechab burst out. Flora shushed her with a finger to her lips, and Rechab dropped her voice to a whisper. "What am I? I am nothing. Nothing that daemons or traders should look at twice."

"Apparently," Flora said, "that is not true. I don't know what you are, Rechab, but you are clearly not nothing."

She heard herself saying the words before she could rethink them. "I wish Alack was here."

"I told you, you cannot look to man to save you."

"Well, I cannot see the Great God. And I am trying to do as you said and run to him."

Flora laid a hand on Rechab's shoulder and squeezed. "It's all right. I am frightening you; I am sorry. My brother did us a boon by telling me of his suspicions; we will journey as planned, but I will have a watch posted at all times behind us so we will know if Amon is indeed coming and if he tries anything. My men are equal to a fight. And I will see to it that we have a plan to get you away if necessary."

"I can't go on without you!" Rechab protested.

"Let us pray you do not have to. I will not send you away alone; don't fear. Don't fear."

Rechab closed her eyes and nodded, repeating the words to herself. She hated the fear that rose up in her gut, twisting and paralyzing and panicking her. Don't fear. Don't fear.

Not even if there is everything to be afraid of.

RACHEL STARR THOMSON

Alack paced in determined circles until Kol Abaddon finally showed up again, midafternoon of the next day.

"I need you to explain something to me!" he cried before the prophet had even drawn near enough to hear a normal tone of voice. "I need you to tell me!"

Kol Abaddon looked impassively at him from under bushy eyebrows. "Something has happened to you."

"Yes, something has happened!"

"Another vision?"

"I don't know . . . maybe. Can one *feel* visions?"

Kol Abaddon positioned himself on a rock. He looked curious— more interested, in fact, than Alack had ever seen him before. That was gratifying.

"Tell me," the prophet said.

"I slept here where you left me," Alack said, "and awoke to the sound of a sheep bleating. The moonlight was strong, and I am a shepherd, so I followed the sound. It took me into a wadi that cut through the desert floor—see, my arms and legs are scratched by the trees that grew there."

"I see," the prophet said.

"I found a lamb at the end of the wadi," Alack went on. "A perfect white lamb. It was trembling with fear, so I spoke to it and calmed it until I could pick it up, and then I held it until it ceased shaking and I carried it out of the wadi."

"Go on."

"When I came out, jackals surrounded the mouth of the wadi. I could see their eyes on every side."

He said the last with such a triumphant, point-proving note

that Kol Abaddon sat back and folded his arms defensively. "Well?"

"Well! I could not put the lamb down without losing it to the jackals, but neither could I fight with the lamb in my arms. So what could I do? I was trapped there."

He threw himself down in the dust, sitting cross-legged and looking accusingly up at the prophet. "And then it all simply disappeared. The jackals, the lamb, all of it. I spent all morning looking for the wadi, and can I find it? I cannot, though my arms and legs are scratched and I have lost my staff somewhere. In a wadi that is nowhere. Was that a vision, Kol Abaddon?"

"That," the prophet said slowly, "was something I cannot interpret for you."

Alack closed his eyes and let out a heavy breath of air—relief or frustration, he wasn't sure which. "I thought you would tell me it was a dream, and that I imagined it all and scratched myself sleepwalking."

"Do you think that is what happened?"

"I know it is not."

"Then why would I tell you it was?"

"Most people would."

"I am not most people."

"No." He hugged his knees to his chest and frowned. "So it was from the Great God, what I saw."

"Most assuredly."

"But you cannot tell me what it was or how to interpret it."

"You must ask those questions of the Great God yourself."

"I have been doing nothing but asking!"

"Ah," said Kol Abaddon, "but asking yourself, or asking the God?"

Alack stopped to think that one over. Perhaps, if he was truly honest with himself, he would have to admit that he had not stopped to ask his questions of the God but only paced and searched and flung his questions around his own mind.

"The Great God knows your thoughts," Kol Abaddon said. "But he likes to be addressed."

And that was the last thing the prophet said that day. At least he did not disappear again. Hunger gnawed at Alack's insides, so he trekked into the wilderness a little way and gathered what food he could find— broad cactus that could be cut open and sucked and a rock dove that he killed with a stone from his slingshot. He found a nest of beetles but refused to raid it. Soon he would eat like a madman, but he saw no reason to start while he could still find fowl. He brought his prey triumphantly back to the olive tree and the spring, but Kol Abaddon ignored it—until Alack had finished roasting it over a fire, at which point the prophet helped himself to a generous portion without a word of recognition or thanks. Alack raised an eyebrow but said nothing. And people thought shepherds were ill-mannered.

He could still feel the chill of fear and remember the clear awareness that had seized him in the moonlight at the mouth of the wadi. That he could not put the lamb down without sacrificing it, but neither could he protect it while it was still in his arms.

Kol Abaddon was close enough to hear, but Alack decided he didn't care, and so he formed words and spoke them aloud. "Great God, you have given me a . . . a vision. And I do not understand it. Please show me what I am supposed to see."

Late that night, Kol Abbadon howled.

The sound woke Alack out of a sound sleep and sent chills all through his body as he looked frantically around and spotted the wild man silhouetted against the moon, pacing a high ridge and wailing and beating his chest.

"I do not know you at all," Alack whispered. "And I came so far to follow you. Who are you, Kol Abaddon?"

But of course there was no answer. The Voice of Destruction simply howled his torment into the night. Alack lost the ability to discern between sleeping and waking, his dreams like his waking hours filled with the prophet's cries.

In the morning he wanted to ask about it, but he did not.

Instead he left a wide berth around Kol Abaddon. He realized what was expected of him, though it had not been said, and again he went out and found food and brought it back and cooked it for his mentor, stepping back and watching without comment as Kol Abaddon took the greater share and wolfed it down. Only when he was done eating did Alack come and finish what he had roasted—today, the remnant was one small egg.

His request of the night before, the one made to the Great God himself, went unanswered. He wondered if he should expect an answer to come at a later time and what form it would take—if he would hear a voice, or see a vision, or if he would simply be filled with wisdom and understanding. He wanted to ask Kol Abaddon and felt that doing so was his right as a disciple, but he did not ask, because he could not remove the memory of the night before from his mind.

He had heard the wild man many nights in the wilderness, from the slopes and the pastures where he tended his sheep alongside Naam and the other shepherds of Bethabara and surrounding towns. And he had seen the prophet at the well and even spoken to him. But never had the two images—of the prophet at the well and the tormented howler in the night—come so closely together.

He hoped he would grow accustomed to it, but for now he accepted the strangeness and kept his distance, and his questions to himself.

Once again, as he often did, Kol Abaddon disappeared early in the day, without a word of explanation or instruction as to what Alack was to do with himself while he waited.

This time, at least, he anticipated dinner. And he had no mysterious wadi to search for. So he set out in search of more eggs or a bird, and kept a sharp eye out for a tree that might yield him a replacement staff.

If not for that sharp eye, he might not have spotted his own staff on the ground near . . . he blinked. Surely it could not be.

Yet it was. He darted to his staff, knelt down and picked it up, felt its familiar weight and grain in his hand—and stared into the mouth of the deep, narrow wadi he had spent all the day before trying to find.

It had not been here. He had come this way and thoroughly swept the ground for a mile around.

Yet, here it was. Here he was. And here was his staff, as though to assure him with its solid nature that he was not dreaming or seeing things.

Never mind that he had not dropped the staff at the wadi's mouth—he was sure of that. As far as his memory could tell, he must have dropped it deep within, when he went to pick up the lamb.

This time the wadi was silent, except for the faintest trickle where the tiny stream flowed through the cleft of the ground. He could see no sign of the lamb, nor of the jackals that had surrounded and menaced them in that moment that still was not dulled in his memory.

His pulse raced now as he realized this place was a work of the Great God, and if he had found it again, it was for a reason.

It was then he heard it: a voice calling for help.

Faint, but clearly coming from within the wadi. His heart pounding now, he tightened his fist around his staff and headed into the deep canyon.

As his feet touched the floor by the trickling stream, he heard the voice more clearly, and knew it.

It was Rechab.

"I'm coming!" he shouted, and charged headlong down the wadi.

This time the canyon seemed twice as long as it had in the moonlight. Its steep sides nearly met at the top, casting the whole place into cool shadow; once again, trees and scrub tore at his arms and legs as he pushed through them, rushing heedlessly toward Rechab's cry.

As he went, over the pounding of his own heart in his ears and the call for help that sounded like the loudest thing in the universe, he heard the snarling and snapping of jackals, and then over that, a deep, breathy sound that made his heart stop entirely—

There was a dragon in the wadi.

He had nearly reached the end, but the tight V that was the far end of the canyon was so deeply cast in shadow that he could only just make out Rechab's form, crouching with her hand thrown up to protect her from . . .

Something.

He threw himself forward with a shout.

And blinked up at the blue desert sky.

He was lying on his back in the hard dirt of a shallow valley.

"Rechab!" he shouted, and bounded to his feet, thrusting out his staff to drive off the jackals—

That were not there, for he was alone.

Tears of frustration filled his eyes, stinging them in the heat. What had he seen? What had he heard? Where was Rechab? Where *was* she?

"Tell me," Kol Abaddon's voice came from behind him.

He spun around. The prophet stood there with an intensity of expression that made him want to cry again. Like a child.

But he was so worried about Rechab.

"Tell me," Kol Abaddon said. "Tell me what you just saw."

Alack nodded and fought to get control of himself. The prophet stepped closer and reached out a hand, touching the end of Alack's staff and pushing it down. He had not realized he was still brandishing it like a weapon.

"I'm sorry," he said, lowering the staff to the dirt. "I didn't . . ."

"I know. Tell me."

Alack choked out, as best he could, what had just happened. He could still hear her voice. He could still see her, cowering against the walls of the wadi.

When he had finished, and when he had calmed himself enough to interpret what he saw, he was surprised—even shocked—at the expression on the prophet's face. Kol Abaddon was marveling at him.

"You have seen another vision from the Great God," he said, "but these are wondrous visions. In all my days as a wandering holy man I have never once entered into a vision as you have done. Your scratches still bleed."

Alack looked down to see that the prophet spoke true. And now that he paid attention, they still stung as well.

"What does it mean?" Alack asked.

"The vision itself, or the way you experience it?"

"Both."

Kol Abaddon frowned. "The way you experience it—entering into the vision. It tells me the calling on your life is strong. The Great God invites you not only into sight, but into encounter. I have never seen the like."

Alack nodded dumbly, trying to digest that but finding it wasn't easy to do.

"But another thing. You saw first a lamb, then a girl you care for. Even love. Yes?"

"Yes," Alack said, wishing his voice wasn't still shaking.

"So the Great God engages your heart in these visions. That means something. And it may mean you will play a role yourself—maybe you are not only a prophet, but a saviour."

At that, Alack could only stare blankly at his mentor.

Kol Abaddon was the most taciturn person he had ever met—and though Alack did not like to be critical, the prophet also seemed lacking in grace and kindness. Yet he would speak such words, without hesitation.

Such words.

"But that may be wrong," Kol Abaddon said abruptly. "Believe only what the Great God tells you. Time will prove my interpretation for what it is. I am only guessing."

He turned and began to walk away, but paused, and turned his head back.

"Thank you," he said. "For the food."

CHAPTER 8

Rechab was no stranger to desert travel. Her father's trade took him all across the Sacred Land, even to its farthest borders, and she had accompanied him from girlhood. But this time, as she veiled her face against the dust, the sun, and the prying eyes of any who should not see her, everything about the journey felt new.

For the first time, she was not traveling in the retinue of Nadab the Trader. For the first time, the destination was a total mystery to her. And for the first time, she was on the run.

Fleeing for her life or her soul, and she did not know why.

She had tried to press Flora for answers to this, but Flora seemed as uncertain as she, and anyway, the sudden change in all of her plans had left her with a lot on her mind. So Rechab stood by as servants saddled her camel, and she mulled over her future and what might be dogging her steps without insight from anyone else.

The one conviction she discovered in her own heart, sitting down deep like a layer of heavy sediment, was that Nadab was somehow at fault. The daemon had claimed that Rechab was sold to them, and the only person in any position to sell her was Nadab the Trader, her own father.

He would not knowingly sell her into the terror she had glimpsed in the daemonized man, but money would blind any man who was in love with it, and Nadab had known no other love for many, many years.

What Amon's interest in her was she could not guess, but it seemed to her that it must have something to do with his slave's terrifying declaration of ownership. The great man had surely heard about it.

Flora passed through the governor's brass gates in a cloud of activity, surrounded by servants and camel drivers and a small company of the governor's attendants—plus Aurelius and his wife, Marah. Rechab hung back, close to her own camel, as they said their good-byes and bowed and scraped and kissed and blustered. Flora, she noted, could bluster every bit as well as her brother. The whole scene was as much play-acting as anything sincere, but knowing that Aurelius had warned Flora about Amon warmed Rechab's heart toward him more than her wont. He had always governed Bethabara well, even if it was no secret that he looked more to his own reputation in the royal courts than to the welfare of the villagers themselves. Perhaps besides that ability to rule, he also had a heart somewhere.

The commotion culminated in their actual leavetaking, and the road stretched down into the wilderness before them, and soon hours had lapsed to the comfortable rhythm of a camel train. Rechab was positioned somewhere in the middle of the train, surrounded by protection but also comfortably alone with her own thoughts.

Or it would have been comfortable, if her thoughts were not so troubled.

She found herself scanning the desert for some sign of Alack. He had not come to find her at the house, not in days, and she was forced to admit that Flora must be right: he had gone to be discipled by the prophet. It was a hard thing to picture—her childhood friend walking with a madman, trying to hear from the Divine while his steps took him further and further away from anything like a normal life. But then, her life too had taken a sudden and drastic departure from normal.

She wished she knew for sure what had happened to him. She could kick herself now for not seeking out Naam and asking him. But she'd been so sure at first that Alack was just doing his duties as a shepherd, and then, with the scare about Amon, Flora hadn't wanted her to leave.

Rechab, accustomed to doing what she was told and just as accustomed to letting the fear in her gut make her decisions for her, had done what Flora wanted.

She regretted that now.

As the terrain passed beneath her, it struck her sharply that she might not ever come back again.

And if she never came back again, chances were she would never see Alack again.

She had not expected the final separation to come so suddenly.

Just ahead of her camel, a small herd of mules carried burdens. A pair of dogs ran around their feet, kicking up dust and raising a cacophony of braying and protest and barking. She welcomed the distraction.

"They are a noisy lot," said a voice beside her.

She turned her head to see that one of Flora's servants, a fresh-faced, eager-looking young man, had drawn up alongside her camel. She liked the way his eyes laughed at the scene ahead of them.

"Addled, the mules are," he said. In a swift and unexpected motion he had jumped down from his camel and plunged into the little herd, grabbing bridles and bringing order. She watched, entertained and grateful for the diversion. One of the mules fought his direction, and between him yelling at the mule and the mule yelling back, the whole muddle caught the attention of a few other servants, who laughed and called down instructions. The young man jumped around and finally got the best of the mule. Then clapping his hands and calling the dogs to him, he jogged back to his dromedary—which was calmly plodding along as though nothing had happened—and remounted.

"Impressive," Rechab said.

"Yes," he answered, his eyes twinkling. "My mother said you can tell a man by the mastery of his mule. I took it to heart."

"Are the mules yours?" she asked.

"That they are." He tipped his head. "They call me Aaron. Mule master and ass breaker."

"I'm called Rechab," she answered.

"Of course you are," he said, and she got the impression he was trying to peer past her veil. "We all know you."

"Then you pay good attention," she said, "for I had little to do with mule trainers while I was working in the governor's courtyard."

"True enough, but we are all one family while we travel together. And even if your reputation had not carried, Mistress Flora has commanded us all to keep a careful eye on you."

She blushed a little, grateful for the veil. His eye seemed more interested than careful, but she couldn't say she was unhappy about it—the young man was pleasant enough to look at, and more than pleasant to talk to.

His description of the caravan intrigued her. Since Flora had no permanent servants of her own, she had assumed the group had been pulled together somewhat more haphazardly than he seemed to suggest. She said as much.

"Mistress Flora sets out once every year and always draws her retinue from the nearest villages," Aaron answered. "She is quick to dismiss anyone she does not trust and to call a second time on anyone she does. Most of us have traveled together with her five years or more."

"Even you?" Flora asked, surprised.

"Even me. She took me along for the first time when I was only twelve." He pointed at the motley herd in front of them. "For my mules."

"And for your heart," Rechab said. "It seems a good heart."

He blushed, without a veil to hide it. She smiled at his too-honest face—but he did not seem to mind, even if his face reddened even more at her smile. He grinned and rode his camel a little harder, pulling up in front of her.

Her heart felt much lighter.

———◆◆◆———

Alack watched from a rocky pinnacle as a camel train passed below. From this distance he could not see who it was, but it looked like a merchant caravan—one still carrying not a few goods. Strange that such a caravan would be moving this direction. Ordinarily merchants would have taken their merchandise to the Holy City and sold it all there, traveling back with money rather than goods.

He frowned. In the distance behind it, he could see the dust from another group in motion. For some reason the sight gave him pause. Robbers? But the clouds of dust suggested too many riders for that. Robbers were more likely to hide in the rocks and ambush prey than to follow them anyway.

Four days in the wilderness, and he was alone again. He had not expected his apprenticeship to involve quite so much time on his own. But then, his master had been alone for years. Maybe this was just part of the job.

Or maybe Kol Abaddon was just unusually ill-tempered and antisocial.

Even if he was, Alack could not find in his heart to be angry or resentful. Not since the last words the prophet had spoken to him—both the words of simple thanks and the possible interpretation of his vision.

Not just a prophet, but a saviour.

Was that really possible?

Kol Abaddon seemed to think it was.

Alack settled himself against a rock and kept himself occupied by watching the merchants far below. The second dust cloud continued to trail the first, but it did not seem to be gaining on them. Perhaps, after all, it was merely a second train leaving the mountain for reasons of its own.

He closed his eyes and saw giant waves foaming and breaking in a dark, wild sea.

He gasped and opened his eyes again. Kol Abaddon was there, staring at him intently.

This time the prophet didn't have to ask.

"I saw waves," Alack said. "On a storming sea."

The prophet nodded. "I have seen the same. We must go."

"Go? Go where?"

"We are leaving the land."

The words were the last Alack expected to hear. "We—what? What are you talking about?"

Kol Abaddon had already begun to walk away, but this time he clearly expected to be followed. Alack scrambled to catch up with him. "What do you mean, we are leaving the land?"

"I mean what I said. We are leaving."

"But . . . but where are we . . ."

He stopped.

He knew the answer.

"The sea."

"The Westland on the Great Sea, yes," Kol Abaddon said.

"But why?"

"Because I have a message for their king," the prophet answered.

———◆———

The rider came fast, galloping up alongside the camel train in a flurry of dust and drawing abreast of Flora at the front of it. A hurried and whispered conversation ensued. Rechab had moved up in the ranks a little and was close enough to observe the encounter, but not to hear anything that was said or catch Flora's response. The rider took off again in the direction he had come only moments later, and she watched him go and then urged her camel forward.

Flora rode in state, aboard a litter on camelback. She had offered one to Rechab, who hadn't wanted to take her up on it. But now, as she drew near, the shaded interior and silk cushions within seemed enviable.

Flora saw her coming and drew the sheer curtains aside. "There you are," she said.

"That messenger . . . did he . . ."

"Yes, he came from the posts I have watching behind us." Flora's expression was clearly troubled. "Amon is indeed following us, though he does not seem to be in any great hurry."

"What does that mean?"

"My guess? That he is biding his time, keeping within range until he can attack somewhere farther away from witnesses or help."

The words were chilling. "And we do not yet know why he follows."

Flora waved her hand. "What reason does he need? I am a woman of wealth, but I do not have much power beyond that. It's a wonder I wasn't robbed and killed long ago."

Something sharp flashed in her eyes as she spoke, and Rechab became suddenly aware of the way Flora's entire retinue seemed poised for something—and armed, she realized. And ready.

"It's a dangerous world," Flora said. "I make it my business to be prepared. Here, climb up here."

Looking both ways as though someone was likely to object, Rechab made the awkward switch from one camelback to the other. Inside, she unwrapped her veil and leaned back with a sigh.

"More comfortable than you would think, isn't it?" Flora said. "I am not a luxurious woman, but I try to make use of a few amenities while I am still far from home. The closer I get to Essea, the more of these trappings I shed."

She spoke with the half-smile that Rechab was coming to know well, one that laughed both at herself and at the world. The strangest person Rechab had ever met, Flora Infortunatia was also perhaps the most self-aware, and the savviest about the world around her. Rechab marveled again at what odds had picked her up and placed her in Flora's company—more than that, in her favour.

Almost as if she could read her mind, Flora said, "Do you know why I wanted you to work for me?"

Rechab shook her head.

"Maybe you are thinking it was luck," Flora said. "It was nothing of the kind. I chose you. There is a wise saying: Nothing happens by accident. Relationships especially do not happen by accident; they are always a matter of choice. I chose you because when you snuck into my brother's house and eavesdropped on my audience with the prophet, you gasped when I spoke of the darkness in the Holy City."

Rechab nodded. She remembered that—the involuntary sound she'd made was the whole reason Flora had known she and Alack were there.

"And," Flora went on, "I am a friend to any heart that hates the darkness. So I determined to step in and to help you escape that darkness in any way I could. But listen to me, Rechab . . . you have to step up yourself. You can't just trade one fear for another, or go from expecting one man to arrange your future to hoping another man will do it. It's not enough just to hate and fear darkness. You also have to love and seek light."

"Run to the Great God," Rechab said, "as you are always telling me."

"Yes," Flora said, frowning. She looked a bit like a child whose will had been crossed. "But you still are not doing that. You are running away, but you don't have much choice, and it's me you're looking to, not the Great God."

Rechab looked away, half-smiling at Flora's vexation and forward manner. It was hard to know exactly how to respond to such a lecture—with anger? With laughter? She'd never known anyone to be so frank.

She decided to try to answer with equal frankness—though before her first words had come out her mouth, she knew she couldn't. She didn't know herself well enough.

Still, she said, "I don't know how to run to the Great God. I don't how to seek him. He's invisible."

"That doesn't mean he's not present."

"Maybe. Or maybe he is gone. Maybe the idols and the shadow

in the Holy City have driven him completely away. Or maybe he has left us in anger and is sending the prophet's terrible army upon us to destroy the last of our people so he will never have to think of us again. How can you know, when you cannot see him?"

Flora looked at her with her head tilted, curiously, but she seemed happier with Rechab now—in this more unguarded moment.

"All of that could be true, if the Great God never spoke," she said. "If we are just guessing, anything could be true. For that matter, he could be dead. But we are not just guessing. He is not silent, and he is not inactive."

"When have you ever heard him?" Rechab asked.

"I have heard the prophet speak. The prophet has seen visions. And others in our community—sometimes they hear."

"And that is all."

"There are writings. Laws. The priests have them, though it has been many years since they taught them to the People."

"Well, I have also heard the prophet. He tells us that the Great God's army is coming to destroy us all, that nothing will stand against them. That they are like locusts filling the air and swarming over the ground, and that they will run up the walls of the Holy City and come in at the windows and slay the People wherever they are found. That is what the Great God promises. So I am not sure why I should run to him, instead of simply being more afraid and trying to run . . . somewhere else."

She thought she sounded like a petulant child at the end, but she hadn't realized she felt as strongly as she did until she said the words. The Holy City belonged to the Great God, didn't it? And she was never more terrified than when she was there.

To her surprise, Flora seemed to be seriously considering something she had said. "You think the prophet comes just to express the

Great God's anger?" she asked.

"What else?"

"To warn us. To give us a chance—a choice."

"What choice?"

"The choice to turn back. The choice to turn away destruction." Flora tapped her chin in thought. "In Essea, they teach that as mankind, we always have a choice until it is too late, and the Great God always shows us that choice so that in nothing are we ever truly innocent or powerless. We always have a part in making our own destiny."

Rechab laughed bitterly. "Like I do? I am a trader's daughter. I have no choices. My father will sell me to whom he will and I will go where my husband says go and that is the end of it."

"You say that, and yet here you are."

"Where you brought me."

"Yes, and look at me. They call me Infortunatia—the Unlucky. I am the illegitimate child of a family that hates me, I lost two husbands, and I cannot even enjoy the wealth I gained because my heart drives me to the wilderness to seek an invisible God. Call me unlucky if you will, but I make choices. And I made them long before I inherited all this or gained the power to decide where I would go and what I would do. I made them as a child when I ran from the abomination Kimash, and I made them as a young woman when I decided I would love my husbands—both of them—although they were old and ugly, and I make them now even though I am running through the wilderness from a man who may attack at any time and try to take my life from me. The choices may not be great and they may not be immediately obvious, but they are always here, and they are always making me. The choices make me—far more than the circumstances that I tend to think are the greater force."

Rechab stared at her. "That is a wise saying," she answered finally.

Flora laughed. "Good. You can repeat it sometime."

She poked her head outside of the litter and called for one of the guards riding nearby. "Any sign of trouble?" she asked.

"Nothing. Someone watching us from a high ridge—but only a shepherd, I think. He has made no move."

Flora leaned back and let the curtains drift closed. "Good," she said. "Let us hope the peace will keep."

CHAPTER 9

Flora's merchant train traveled until the sun had nearly reached the horizon. They had come to a protected valley, with sharp, sheer cliffs of red rock on either side that would allow no one to come at them from above and a broad exit into a complex landscape that would allow multiple paths of escape—and many places to hide. Rechab marveled that Flora and her company had known exactly when they would reach this place and pushed their day's journey late in order to obtain it. She had grown nervous sometime back, eager to stop and make camp before dark. But she admired their wisdom and superior knowledge now. Rarely had she ever traveled east with her father, as most of his dealings lay in other regions; this place was strange to her. At the same time, she realized that even if she did know it, she might never have viewed it from a defensive perspective. It was clear that Flora was accustomed to warding off attack, or at least to planning for it.

The arms of her men had grown more evident as the day lengthened. Suddenly Rechab was seeing scimitars and spears, hatchets and bows, not merely daggers and staffs. This company of servants and slaves, it seemed, was outfitted as a small army.

The sight might have been enough to alleviate her fears entirely, were it not for the strain she could see in their faces. That indicated that however strong they might be, they expected Amon to be just as strong—or stronger.

At least in their resting place, they had made void the chance of a surprise attack. Amon's men could come from only one direction, and the valley entrance was too narrow for Flora's sharp-eyed scouts to miss anyone trying to approach. Soon there were watchfires burning and meat roasting and tents standing as shadows against the valley walls; the camels were staked and tended to, and Rechab found herself wandering the narrow lanes of the camp, hugging herself against the chilling air and missing home intensely.

She would never see her father again, or her elder brothers and sisters, or the servants who had been like family. She had not processed any of that until now. Here, under a starry sky, with the threat of attack on their heels.

The words of the daemonized slave kept shrieking in her ears: You have been sold to us.

Everything she knew wrested from her—her life so completely out of her control.

And yet, she could not help thinking about what Flora had said.

Did she, even here, have a choice?

Could she make any difference to her own future? Or to her own soul in the journey?

Maybe that was the more important question. Not whether she could influence what would happen to her, but whether she could have any say in who she became.

Here, torn away from everything she knew and staring into a future that was formless and frightening, that seemed more important than it ever had before.

RACHEL STARR THOMSON

She had left the past behind. There was no going back. So there was no question that she too would change. She had to.

The men talked in low voices at the campfires along the hastily made paths, and as she wandered she let herself pick up pieces of their conversations—names, laughter, references to home. Though they all traveled together, not one of these was a wanderer like she was.

Not one had a future that was an entirely open door, without much hint of what could possibly lie on the other side.

A loud braying and cursing from the other side of the camp drew her attention and made her laugh, and minutes later Aaron came cutting between tents, wiping his brow and shaking his head, muttering something under his breath.

"Still stubborn?" she asked.

"Always," he said. "Are you hungry? Come, sit and eat something."

He ushered her to the nearest fire, where an older man was crouched down turning a piece of meat on a spit. Goat, she thought. The man made room for her without fuss, a kindness she appreciated more than she could say. She knew she could join Flora at any time and be welcomed, but Rechab wasn't sure she liked making a distinction between herself and the others, who were all clearly Flora's hired servants, and anyway, she was not sure how much conversation with the daughter of Florus Laurentinus her conflicted soul could take in one day. Flora had shown herself a true friend and had probably saved Rechab's life, but she was intense.

By contrast, Aaron and the older man—Joachim—talked about mules and goat meat and the weather and what they were going to do when they got home, and Rechab found the chatter comforting. Neither seemed to mind in the least that she was there, or to regard her as an interloper.

They quieted as one of the watchmen passed through the camp

again, headed for Flora's tent. Rechab watched him threading his way through the fires and little huddles of servants, her mind drifting away from her companions' chatter and onto more serious things once more.

When the watchman exited the tent, Flora followed. She looked this way and that, and spotting Rechab, came over to her and sat down at the fire. Aaron and the older man exchanged a quick glance and then excused themselves.

"Is something wrong?" Rechab asked.

"No," Flora said. "Quite the opposite. The watchmen report that Amon is gone."

"Gone?" Rechab echoed, surprised. "Has he gone ahead—to ambush us further down the road?"

"It seems not. He's gone south—the way to his own homeland in the plains. Some of my men are still following to ensure he doesn't double back, but it looks as though he's left off following us."

"But why?" Rechab asked.

Flora shrugged, but she looked more thoughtful than her confident tone implied. "Perhaps he decided we weren't as vulnerable as he thought. That is true, in any case. Every man in my company can put up a good fight; attacking us would have cost Amon dear even if he had won the day."

Flora reached out and touched Rechab's arm. "You are well? Content with your lodgings? Comfortable?"

"Yes," Rechab said, managing a smile. "I'm sorry I've been so . . . distant."

"That's all right. You're dealing with a lot. And I am not always good at leaving space to think and feel; I know that."

The apology was real—Flora sounded slightly ashamed of herself. Rechab's heart went out to her. It was not as though she had done anything wrong. Entirely the opposite—Rechab owed the woman her life.

"You have been a good friend," she said. "My recalcitrance is my own fault, not yours."

Flora smiled. "Thank you for saying that, even if you don't believe it fully. I am glad the hunter is off your trail, if indeed that is the case."

———◆◆———

Days passed and Flora's watchmen confirmed that Amon had gone south and posed no more threat to them. The confirmation lifted a weight Rechab hadn't known she was still carrying, and she breathed easier.

The days fell into a rhythm that might have been monotonous if Rechab hadn't taken an interest in all of the servants, with their personalities and their histories, but she did, and watching and listening to them helped her pass the time. The wilderness too was beautiful, even in its barrenness, and Flora never ceased to be interesting.

True to her word, Flora shed more and more of her finery as they traveled closer to the desert community where she lived, selling it or leaving it in villages and with clusters of merchantmen camped in oases that Flora clearly frequented. Two days from Essea, she had left behind all but three servants, traded her silks and linen for unadorned homespun, wrapped herself in a plain veil, and retained of her beasts only a stubborn mule and its sister, saddled for herself and Rechab to ride. One of the servants was Aaron, and Rechab gathered the mules were his and would go with him when they had no more use for them.

Essea lay before them, and Rechab trembled at the newness of the life it represented. Flora had tried to describe the place and its ways—

where everyone was as a servant and no one as a master, where prayers and fasting made up a great deal of the work of every day and where the other work was in studying laws and prophecies and working with their hands. It sounded austere, a little fanatical, and not at all welcoming.

"I know they will allow you to stay as long as you wish," Flora told her as they hobbled along on muleback, "as a refugee. And if you desire to become a pilgrim like us, they will welcome you."

She knew Flora hoped that she would embrace the latter calling, but the idea struck her soul like the plucking of an instrument with dread and a note of despair. The colourful life she had initially hoped for in Flora's employ—full of interesting work and fascinating people, riches and feasting and merchandise, status and responsibility—the life she was suited for as a trader's daughter and which in fact she loved—had been replaced by something dry and lifeless.

Flora seemed to recognize that. "It is not so terrible as it sounds," she said, with her eyes uncharacteristically cast down. "There is a spiritual life that is rich and beautiful, only heightened by the poverty of our surroundings. We give up everything to gain everything. That is our calling and our way."

Yet this Flora, stripped of all accoutrements and ready to enter the life she had chosen again, did not seem more alive or more beautiful. Her manner was more subdued—almost shamed.

Rechab did not like it.

They reached a small village, far tinier than Bethabara, and here Aaron and the other two servants said farewell. Flora and Rechab handed over their mules, and Flora pulled her veil over her face. "We are nearly there," she said.

Together they walked the last mile to the community. Though the land here was flatter than at home, and more monotonous, it dipped into a lower plain where a slow-moving river twisted past, and there by the water Rechab caught her first glimpse of the chosen home of Flora the Unlucky.

A stone wall surrounded the community of Essea, eight feet in height, and gated with iron. The gates were ornate—more so than anything else in sight—engraved with the faces of an eagle and a lion. Though Flora said nothing about it, Rechab wondered if she had contributed the iron and the metalwork from her own mines and resources.

On the inside, the compound housed one long building of whitewashed stone, with narrow windows cut all down its length. Here Rechab assumed the community gathered for some purpose, or perhaps many. Besides that were small brick huts where the people could sleep, all of them tiny and lacking in any ornamentation, and the usual ovens and cisterns in the yard. The whole compound was oval in shape.

"That is our sanctuary," Flora said, pointing to the long hall. "There we go to pray. There too, we study the words of the Great God together and hear what any prophets or teachers will say."

"I thought you might eat together there," Rechab said.

"We did once, but in recent years we practice solitude more and more. Most eat in their own huts."

Once again Rechab found herself wondering how Flora could thrive here—how anyone could.

As they approached, a horn blew two long blasts.

"That is the call to convene in the long hall for study," Flora said. "The Teacher will speak to us all now. It is a good time for us to arrive—I can announce my return and introduce you."

She withdrew her veil enough to smile with her eyes. "Don't be afraid," she said. "Our ways are strange, but everyone here is a good man or a good woman. We seek the Great God together, and he blesses us. You are both safe and welcome here."

Rechab nodded, though the old knot of fear was bunching in her stomach again. It did not help that this more subdued version of Flora was something of a stranger. As overwhelming as Flora the merchant could be, Flora the pilgrim was unknown, and far less a pillar of strength.

They passed through the iron gate without even a guard to stop them and went straight to the doors of the long hall, which was only fifty paces from the gate. They entered without challenge or fanfare. The air within was cloying with incense and smoke. Light came in through high windows, too high to see outside, and now that they were closer Rechab could see the windows were carved in the form of religious symbols—stars, clusters of grapes, and grains of sand in a peculiar pattern that was indicative of the Holy People. The largest window, at the far end of the hall, was an eye: open, watching.

The eye of the Great God.

Rechab shivered.

Nearly one hundred of Flora's fellow pilgrims were packed into the hall, all on their knees, all with their backs to the newcomers. They faced the end of the hall and the eye. Their posture at this moment was facedown to the floor, and without a word, Flora dropped to her own knees behind them and affected the same posture.

Rechab, not sure what to do, followed suit.

As she bowed her forehead close to the floor, shutting out her view of all but the shadows and the floor itself, she became aware of something she had never felt before.

She could only describe it as a Presence.

She was kneeling before—something. Someone.

Her body trembled from head to foot, but not with the usual fear. This was a special fear all its own—a response to the presence of one who was watching, who was listening, who knew all, and who required much.

The hall was full of murmuring, the whispered prayers of the gathered pilgrims. Rechab could not join their voices. She did not know what to say.

She could only kneel and tremble and know that her soul was bared and barren before the eye of the Great God.

Some time passed, and a sonorous voice said, "You may rise."

A general shuffle ensued as the worshipers straightened and changed their posture to a crouch or a cross-legged seat on the floor. Rechab joined them, red-faced and glad she and Flora were at the back of the room where no one could see that she did not really know what she was doing.

At the far end of the hall, through the hazy shadows, light fell on a tall man dressed all in white. He was unremarkable except for his height, but when he spoke, his voice was deep and commanding.

"Welcome home, Flora," he said. Heads turned and nodded to them as Flora stood.

"You have brought us a guest?"

"Yes, Teacher," Flora said. She held out her hands to Rechab, who stood and inched closer to her friend, hating the knot in her stomach and her acute discomfort at being the center of attention here. She was used to being on display in Nadab's tents, and had felt no lack of ease managing affairs for Flora in Aurelius's house, but this place was totally foreign, and she had no status or understanding with these people.

"This is Rechab," Flora said. "She needs a place of safety, and I told her she would be welcome here."

The tall man inclined his head. "As indeed she is. You may shelter here, Rechab, as long as you have need and are willing to abide in our ways."

"Yes," Rechab stammered out. "I thank you."

She and Flora stayed standing a minute longer while all eyes in the room got a good look at them. She was grateful when Flora at last indicated for her to sit.

"I trust your travels were satisfactory," the Teacher said. It took Rechab a moment to realize he was still addressing Flora, although she was seated.

"Indeed, Teacher," she said. She said nothing more—which Rechab found odd, considering the abrupt ending to Flora's business and the early return to Essea. But the Teacher did not ask to know more.

"You will do the usual penance," the Teacher said. "To wash away the stains of the world."

"Yes," Flora responded.

From there the Teacher went on into a discussion which Rechab could barely follow. He read from a scroll and spoke about its contents—but it was all measurements and materials and instructions for building, and Rechab could not tell what structure was meant or why anyone should be so interested in it. The strong sense of a presence had left as soon as she came off her knees and lifted her face from the floor, but the eye overhead still made her nervous, and she longed for the moment she could step outside of the hall and back into the sun.

That moment came soon enough. The oration ended after forty minutes or so, and as she and Flora were near the back of the hall, Rechab was one of the first to emerge blinking into the sunlight. Some of the women scattered to the ovens, and within minutes the smell of flat bread baking filled the air. A welcome, homey smell.

She looked around for Flora, who had inexplicably disappeared right after exiting the hall, and found her to one side of the long building tying something to her hands. Weights, Rechab realized upon closer inspection.

RACHEL STARR THOMSON

"What are those?" she asked.

Flora looked up at her with a smile—but the smile did not reach her eyes. "These are my penance," she said. "For three nights I will worship with weights on my hands, so that I may recall the weight of the world beyond this place and the heaviness of my sins and long for the lightness of pure worship and forgiveness."

"But you did nothing wrong out there," Rechab said.

Flora gave her a warning look. "It is easy to become tainted by the world. A pilgrim needs a pure heart."

Rechab wanted to keep insisting—But you did nothing wrong. I do not see why you should suffer for having conducted yourself righteously.

But she did not say anything. She was still too new here, and too bound by the Teacher's insistence that she "abide in their ways." Maybe not questioning the Teacher was one of their ways. Or maybe she just did not understand what this was really all about.

"You will sleep in my hut with me," Flora said, "unless you would rather stay in the guest quarters. But there are others there."

Two nights ago Rechab would have opted for the guest quarters. But she felt something she had not felt for Flora before—pity.

So she said, "I will stay with you."

Flora flashed a quick and genuine smile. "I am glad. I think I can teach you to understand this place. Perhaps even to love it."

She led the way along the length of the hall toward a cluster of huts in the far end of the compound. "I sleep in the wall," she said. Now that they drew closer, Rechab could see that some of the huts, rather than free standing, were built into the wall itself. "I will show you, and then we will come and find supper and eat. It has been a long journey."

"What did the Teacher mean by abiding in your ways?" Rechab asked.

"Only that you respect our way of life and do not interfere with it. No immorality is tolerated within our walls, and times of prayer must be respected. But you are free to join in or not, and to attend our meetings or not. And you may wander the compound and the lands around us freely." Flora hesitated. "Though I would not go out of the walls alone. If I were you. Just . . . given the circumstances of your coming here."

"I understand," Rechab said, her heart sinking. She did understand, and she agreed. But she wondered how long the possibility of threat would loom over her head and keep her locked in places she did not want to be.

"That scroll he read," Rechab said. "All those instructions. What building was he talking about? And who is building it? Will the people of Essea raise it up?"

Flora looked at her with a mix of sadness and curious recognition. "The building already exists," she said; "it was raised long ago. The scroll he read were the blueprints given by the Great God himself."

"The Great God? But what building did he ever . . ."

"The temple in Shalem," Flora answered. "The Great God gave all his instructions for it through a prophet in the old days."

"I didn't know," Rechab said, wondering. Her memories of the temple in earlier days were good—its grand height, its golden roof and doors and altars, its beautiful mosaics and engravings and its veils and curtains of purple and crimson. In recent years that grandness had been clouded in her mind by the darkness in the Holy City and the fear that bound her every time she stepped foot there. The beautiful temple had become, in its own way, a place of horror to her.

"Yes," Flora said. "We read those ancient scrolls to remember that the Great God once loved Shalem and set his name and his presence there. To remember that the temple was a holy place, the great sanctuary, before the idols defiled it and the People forgot their true lord."

The thought was unexpectedly sad.

Flora's hut, its outer wall made of the compound wall's solid stone, its roof thatched and its inner three walls built of burnt brick, had just enough space for both women to lay out a mat and sleep. Two mats, woven from rushes, leaned against one wall.

"Two?" Rechab asked.

"I have sometimes had other guests. One recently, just before I made my journey. She did not stay long, but perhaps the Great God was preparing this space for you."

The roof thatching was light and let in some of the sunlight, as did an opening in one of the brick walls. A piece of tanned skin hung beside the opening, ready to be drawn across it.

"This is where I sleep and also where I pray," Flora said. "My prayer habits you already know—three times a day. You are welcome to join me, but I think you might rather take those times to walk. Many of the women go down to the river, and you can accompany them. The community also keeps a watch out as well."

"I meant to ask you about that," Rechab said. "We came into the compound without even being stopped. Are the gates always open?"

"No," Flora said. "We have eyes. You will not see them, but there is always a watch posted, and they will see and stop anyone who tries to come in who is unwelcome. They know me, and they know I will not bring a threat into the community. So we were able to enter unmolested."

Rechab nodded—happier with the idea of going beyond the walls if she knew someone would be looking out for her. Flora's earlier advice still held; she would only go out in groups with the other women. But it was much better than nothing.

She hesitated to ask another question, but Flora saw the hesitation and prompted her to go on.

"When I said to you that the Great God is invisible and we cannot even know if he is still with us—and you said we could read his words and hear from the prophets."

"Yes?"

"Can you also sometimes feel him?" Rechab asked. "His presence—when you pray—"

"There is power and beauty in the spiritual life," Flora said. "Did I not tell you that? Some say it is because we are being lifted to a higher state. Others say it is the presence of the Great God himself we feel. I do feel something. And I know that he hears me."

And sees you, Rechab thought, but she did not add that. She couldn't tell, from Flora's answer, whether her experience in the long hall was something others also experienced or if it had been a special grace.

CHAPTER 10

A lack knew the moment he stepped beyond the boundaries of where he had ever been as a shepherd. Herdsmen roamed far and wide with their flocks and herds, always seeking pasture and shelter and water, and periods of drought would push them farther out than normal. But this far he had never come, and nor had his father before him, nor his father before him.

They were pushing to the far western edge of the Sacred Land.

He missed his sheep. This trek was long and mostly unvarying, the only real interest having to do with when and how Alack would manage to find supper, or whether they would do without it. Kol Abaddon rarely spoke; something was raging behind his eyes that was even more intense and tempestuous than normal. Alack suspected it was the message he had to give to the king of the Westland, but he did not know, as Kol Abaddon did not tell him. There was little difference, in fact, between traveling alone and traveling with the prophet, except that the prophet seemed to have miraculously little need for either rest or water, and Alack suffered for lack of both. He tried not to complain.

He wished he knew whether he were conducting himself well. It was so hard to tell, and he had no example of a good prophet's disciple to measure himself against. "See to your duties," his father had always told him—it was Naam's principal philosophy in life—so Alack put his mind and strength to scrounging up food as often as he could. It was the only duty he could make out, other than trying to keep his eyes and ears open for the Great God.

But then, it seemed visions would find him rather than the other way around. So he didn't know how to measure himself in that respect either.

Kol Abaddon began walking before the sun was completely up and often did not stop until it had set again and cast darkness over the desert. Before then, Alack could see a growing agitation coming over him as the day gave way to evening and shadows crept closer. There had not been any howling episode since this journey began, but he suspected the torment was always right there, ready to seize on the man who called himself the Voice of Destruction.

As they lay down to sleep between a natural ring of boulders in the darkness, somewhere Alack suspected was nearly the exact border of the Sacred Land, he stared up at the stars and remembered his first meeting with Kol Abaddon.

Flora Infortunatia had been wrong. The prophet was not a man after all.

Alack wondered if he would lose all semblance of humanity too. He wondered if knowing the Great God did that to you.

He should ask, he thought.

Not that the God had answered his last question.

He wondered why he had thought it was so important to come out here and follow the prophet—more important than anything.

But even wondering, he knew he would never go back.

Rechab woke in the darkness of the little hut and saw that Flora was praying. Three times a day had been a slight misnumbering; Flora also rose three times in the night. This was the third. The first two times, Rechab had simply rolled over and gone back to sleep, exhausted from the journey. But now she pushed herself up a little on her elbow and watched her friend.

Flora knelt as she prayed, and she was holding her hands up—but they wavered, and Rechab could hear pain in the way she breathed.

The weights.

Rechab had forgotten about them.

Her eyes filled with tears suddenly. Flora had given everything—more than many people would ever possess—to devote her life to seeking the Great God. She had indeed made choices. Painful, sacrificial choices. And was this how she was repaid?

But maybe, Rechab thought, there were mysteries here too deep for criticism.

Maybe she just did not understand.

Yet she couldn't just return to sleep while Flora labored this way.

Quietly moving to sit up, Rechab came behind Flora and placed her hands under Flora's elbows, lifting both her arms.

Flora made a small sound, and in the moonlight Rechab could just see the glitter of tears on Flora's face. She did not know if they had been there before.

Flora prayed in a barely audible mutter that Rechab could not imitate, but while she was here, hands raised under Flora's, kneeling behind her, she knew she ought to pray also.

Pray to the Great God who had looked upon her in the long hall.

Flora said he could hear the thoughts of men's hearts.

So Rechab offered her prayers silently.

I am not devoted as Flora is, she prayed. But I acknowledge that you saw me today. And I thank you that I am alive.

She struggled to put words together, silent though they were. I have been bitter and angry and I am still very afraid. But you saw me. I felt your presence. And I offer you what few of the People give anymore—worship.

That was all.

Yet she knew she had been heard.

This time she did not tremble.

Flora's hands were heavy, and Rechab did not know how long they stayed there, but her arms and shoulders and back ached by the time Flora moved and they could both go back to sleep.

Flora was gone when she awoke, but Rechab quickly found her again—at the community well, only a few steps from the little cluster of huts where they had slept. She still wore the weights bound to her hands, but she raised her eyes from the water to Rechab and they shone with gratitude.

Rechab thought she would never view Flora as intimidating again.

Flora said nothing, and Rechab wondered if it was because of the other women gathered at the well. None of these spoke to either of them, or to each other; perhaps because, as Flora had said, they "practiced solitude." Yesterday Rechab had gone to the river with some of them and found them much the same: not exactly unfriendly, nor unwelcoming, but quiet and cut off. She thought they seemed very spiritual but not especially happy.

The horn-blown call to gather came again, and Rechab did not bother to go. She was still weary from the journey and not sure she could stay awake through more building codes and instructions. She was drawn by the thought of the eye but overwhelmed at the prospect of cramming into the hall with the entire community again, so she stayed without and lingered near Flora's hut.

So it was that she saw Amon in the courtyard.

She ducked instinctively behind one of the huts, telling herself she was seeing things, and peered cautiously back around the wall.

It was him.

The trader from the Southern Plains was strolling through the compound accompanied by two of the community's men—both of whom wore white tassels on their robes that indicated that, like the Teacher, they were more learned and in a position of greater authority than the other pilgrims. Rechab fought back the fear that rose on the wake of her shock: what was he doing here?

Flora had said they would let no one in who posed a threat to Essea. Yet this man was no worshipper of the Great God. And Flora had certainly considered him a threat.

But he had gone—Flora's lookouts had insisted he had gone south.

Apparently he had fooled them somehow.

Wishing she could slip into the long hall and pull Flora out with her, Rechab forced herself to stay still and strained her ears to hear what the men were talking about. But they were not close, and the snatches of speech she could hear were in another language—the classical language of the Southern Plains, she thought, not the familiar pidgin the traders were accustomed to speaking.

Fighting down panic, she waited until they were out of sight and then slipped into the brick hut and sat with her back against the far wall, head on her knees, just trying to stay calm. Flora could not come back soon enough.

But Flora did *not* come back. The meeting in the long hall dismissed—she could hear many others in the courtyard, and smell the baking bread, and hear some of the community at prayer in their quarters—but Flora stayed away. She thought perhaps she ought to go out and look for her, but she couldn't force herself to move.

What if Amon saw her?

What was he *doing* here, anyway?

This could not be coincidence. He had to be here in connection to her and Flora.

She hated the way her fear trapped her here, in a hut that was barely big enough to stretch out in, but she didn't know what else to do.

After hours, her anticipation of Flora's return turned to frustration and then to worry.

Had something happened to her?

Voices outside told her someone was coming—men, more than one of them.

Amon.

They could not find her here.

She looked around frantically, uselessly. There was nothing here but a pair of woven mats and the skin that covered the window. But that was an idea . . .

The opening in the brick was narrow, but Rechab was small. If she waited until the men were all at the door, on the other side of the house, she could get out without them seeing.

The voices told her they were right there. At any moment they would move aside the curtain that functioned as a door and step inside.

She dashed the skin aside and pushed herself out of the window, ignoring the scrape of brick. No one had seen her.

She fled.

The only place she knew to go was the river. But they would find her there.

Slipping through the iron gates, she kept to the shadows of the wall and followed its line to the far side of the compound. There was a grove of olive trees there, and beyond that, a rocky swath of ground where shadows and boulders might make it hard to see one woman, wrapped in drab homespun, running for her life.

———◆———

Flora chafed against the long scrutiny and drawn-out prayers of her meeting with the Teacher, but she tried not to show it.

His response to her return this time was irregular. Usually he made it clear he wanted to know little to nothing of her affairs outside Essea; all that mattered was that she returned and cleansed herself of any of the world's stain before entering into life as usual again. But this time he wanted reports, confessions—a meeting that dragged on for hours, interspersed as it was with prayers and the affairs of others, to whom he stopped to listen, and with whom he stopped to discuss matters, without dismissing Flora. She supposed it was good for her soul to be so humbled and fairly ignored; it was true enough that in the outer world, where she played the wealthy merchantwoman, no one ever dared ignore her. She gave herself her head in that world because confidence and boldness, even brashness, ensured that no one cheated or underestimated her. And she relished the freedom of it.

But here—this was her true home. Her heart's chosen community. The place where she could seek the Great God despite being a foreigner who could not enter the temple; the place where she knew her prayers were heard and her self-abasement was seen and acknowledged. The place where her spirit grew.

So she should not be impatient, and she should not chafe. Only be quiet and humble and wait.

At long last—Flora's knees and back were aching; she didn't know how long she'd been on her knees, and even with her hands folded in her lap the weights took their tool—she rose at the Teacher's bidding and prepared to go.

"You may remove those," he said, glancing at the weights. "I am satisfied your penance is done. But beware, Flora—guard your heart as carefully as you do your merchandise, lest the heady pleasures of wealth carry you away one of these journeys."

"Yes, Teacher," she said, gratefully untying the weights from her hands. She paused, recalling Rechab in the night and the compassionate help she had offered. Her heart warmed.

"There is one other matter," the Teacher said, calling the words after her as she was about to step out the doors.

She stopped and turned. "Teacher?"

The tall man shuffled toward her in his white robes, not meeting her eyes. She thought he had not meant to share this but had thought better of it—otherwise, why wait until she was on her way out to speak?

"The girl you brought here cannot stay," the Teacher said.

Flora's hand on the door froze. "Teacher?" she said again.

"You know our ways. We bring in no one who is a threat to Essea."

"Rechab is no threat!" Flora said, her voice rising.

"She is a marked woman," the Teacher said. "She will draw others after her. Indeed, she already has. She must leave our walls."

Flora's mind fought to understand, to accept—to hear something other than what he was saying. Something more reasonable, and true to who they were. "We refuse only those who are a threat in themselves," she said. "Only those who bring evil. We do not refuse those who need a place to hide from evil. That has never been our way!"

"Who are you to tell me our ways?" the Teacher snapped. Anger had sprung into his eyes—and she suspected it was matched in her own, though his words slapped her harder than she knew was possible.

"You are here by the grace of the People and the Great God," the Teacher continued. "You should be grateful we allow you to touch our hallowed ground. Must I remind you that you are a stranger—a Hill Woman?"

"No, Teacher, you need not remind me of that," Flora said, her voice tightly controlled. Twin responses of anger and pain flared within her. Her hand was still on the door.

He seemed ashamed of his words, and his manner calmed a little. "That was perhaps harsher than necessary. But I fear, Flora, that your time in the world emboldens your spirit against the ways of the Holy People. Have a care, child." His face was still red, and his breath came fast. "Rechab cannot stay with us. This was not an easy choice to make, but when he came and told us what he did, I knew I could not subject every man and woman in this community to the danger she brings."

"He?" Flora asked. "Who is he?"

The Teacher met her eyes. "The man who lays claim to her life."

Flora burst the door open before her. Chickens scattered, squawking, and dust flew, and through the dust and the feathers, she saw Amon standing not ten feet away, flanked by two of the Teacher's apprentices.

"No," she said. "It cannot be."

She wheeled on the Teacher. "What claim does he make to her? He has none!"

The Teacher disdained to answer. "Flora, you must accept my decision. You did right to flee here, but there is nothing we can do for this girl. You must accept that."

"I do not accept that we must feed to the darkness one who belongs to the light," Flora said.

She knew as she spoke the words, as she allowed them out of her mouth, that her days at the community were numbered.

Unless the Teacher would recognize truth in her words and humble himself before it, she could not imagine that he would allow her to stay. No one had ever challenged him so brazenly before.

And he would not humble himself before her—before Flora the Unlucky, the curse-slayer, the foreigner.

For one wild moment she considered attacking Amon and driving him out of the compound herself. But with what? Her bare hands? He did not seem to be armed, but he had the Teacher and hence the entire community on his side.

And she, alone, standing aginst them.

Alone but for Rechab.

Where was Rechab?

She tore her eyes away from Amon and searched the grounds for any sign of the girl, but she could not see her anywhere. Perhaps she was in the hut.

If Amon had not already gotten to her.

Run to the Great God, Flora had said.

Rechab had almost begun to believe that was good advice. But now, it seemed, she was doomed to run away from him again. For the only place she had ever found the Great God was in the long hall in Essea, and she was putting that behind her as fast as she could.

They had betrayed her to Amon. Perhaps even Flora had done it. That was why she had not come out of the hall—she was in talks with the Teacher, and together they were deciding to turn her over to the man who hunted for her. To the man who was somehow in concert with a daemon of the hills.

This was not a good time of the day to run into the wilderness. It was midday, and the sun beat down mercilessly. The desert sands beneath her feet were scorching, and she was grateful for her sandals— but these she had already torn on the rocks as she raced away.

Her vision swimming with heat and panic, she forced herself to stop running and get beneath the shadow of a rock. It would do her little good to escape with her life only to die of sun exposure. Something dashed away from her feet as she ducked into the little available shadow, and she jumped back—grateful to recognize the disappearing tail of a lizard and not the coils of a snake.

No, it would not do simply to run out here. To let panic and fear drive her. They would drive her quickly to her death.

She leaned against the rough sandstone behind her and wished for the sun's slow descent so that shadows might increase—with the sun directly overhead, there was little release. She had not stopped to gather food or water for her flight, nor did she know whether to chide herself for that or not. She could not last long in the wilderness without either, but then, capture had felt so imminent.

Capture. And why? What possible claim did the Southern Trader have on her? What claim did *anyone* have on her?

Caught up in the intensity of that plea, Rechab did something she had never done before.

She made a choice.

Only the night before, she had bowed herself before the seeing eyes of the Great God. She had acknowledged his greatness and his power and that he saw her and knew her and deserved her worship.

So she would do as Flora had urged her so many times to do. She would do as her ancestors had done and enter into covenant with the Great God.

"I will serve you and no other," she said, and that was all.

The choice was made.

No matter what other gods tried to claim her, no matter who sold her to what slavery, she had chosen her allegiance and it would not change.

And with that choice came strength. Nothing miraculous, nothing that changed a single thing in the moment. But it was strength nonetheless, and Rechab could feel the difference. No longer would she only run from; from now on, she was running *to*. Wherever she fled, the flight would be one toward freedom to worship the deity she had chosen.

She felt as though she ought to get up and continue to somewhere, to journey on in the confidence of her decision. But in actual fact she had nowhere to go, and the sun was still too strong and too dangerous to make travel advisable.

Water. She would need water, and soon. There was still the river—if she remembered the view from the ridge accurately, the river curved around in this direction. If she headed west, she should meet up with it, hopefully beyond the boundaries of the community's watch. True, her chances of being found at the river were higher, but staying free of capture would do her little good if she died of thirst. And the river offered better chance of finding food as well—something growing, or the service of a local fisherman.

She settled deeper into the shadow of the rock, grateful that nothing stirred this time. Listening brought no sound to her ears but that of the warm wind. It felt good and right to have a plan. Move again when the desert has cooled. Stay to the shadows and find the river. Drink, eat, and follow the river northward—

The plan ended there.

Thoughts of Flora panged her heart. Had her friend truly betrayed her? Or had something else kept her absent all of that time? Was she in trouble herself—in need? Perhaps even for helping Rechab?

Rechab thought of the way the Teacher seemed to disdain Flora, and her stomach turned. Surely one who served the Great God could see past appearances to know how fervently Flora's heart worshipped and sacrificed. Surely he should recognize her purity.

Thinking those thoughts dispelled Rechab's fears—no, of course Flora had not betrayed her.

So something else had kept her.

Maybe it was only prayers. Maybe the Teacher had wanted to talk. Maybe Flora knew nothing about Amon's coming. For that matter, maybe even the Teacher was innocent in this. She had no proof the community had given her up to the trader—no proof but the driving fear in her heart and the voices of men outside of Flora's hut.

That was all the proof she needed, she decided.

Wisdom dictated she try to sleep. The less energy she expended now, the better, and likely she would need to follow the river into the night.

CHAPTER 11

A lack could not help but stare—at everything. He had heard of Kasarea, of course. The port city near the mouth of the Great Sea was a matter of legend among all tradesmen. But shepherds had no need for the sea, for ships, or for ports, and besides, Kasarea did not belong to the People. It was a city for the nations, swarming with people of every class and tribe and occupation, speaking a hundred different languages and swindling each other in hybrids of all of them. So strange and varying were the men and women who thronged these streets that even Kol Abaddon hardly drew a second glance.

The surly prophet had said little since they entered the port. He chose a seat by the harbour and watched as the ships came in and out, while Alack sat at his feet and fidgeted with impatience. He could only assume they would take ship; the land where they journeyed was some hundred miles north on the coast of the Great Sea, and they would certainly not get there by sitting here.

Kol Abaddon *did* take the time and effort to hand Alack some coins and send him to the market for provisions. Where he had been carrying money all this time Alack could not guess; he had not thought the prophet could hide anything under the animal skins he wore. Apparently he had been wrong.

Or else the prophet could pull coins out of thin air.

There was enough to outfit them for several days, and acting on his belief that they would soon be taking ship, Alack stocked up. Hard bread, dried fish, three skins of wine, and a bag full of figs. It was hardly gourmet fare, but after days of nothing but warm water and the occasional egg or bird, Alack found the haul cheered him up considerably.

He still had no idea what message Kol Abaddon had for the king of the Westland. He hoped it was not marching orders. The army of the Great God, after all, would come from the land where they were going now. Alack had never imagined taking an active role in the judgment he'd foreseen; if the Great God wanted him to tell the king of the west to send his terrible armies on the Sacred Land, Alack thought he would rebel. Let the Great God strike him dead where he stood; he could not betray his people in such a way.

Whether Kol Abaddon felt the same way, he could not be sure.

He soaked up the comfortable warmth of the coast as he traversed the packed road alongside the sea to the place where Kol Abaddon no doubt still sat waiting. The sea air transformed this locale, giving life to high arching palms and many other plants and cooling the desert air till Alack found he wanted to gulp it into his lungs, drinking up the smell of salt and the sound of the waves. Kasarea itself stank, as all cities did, but here along the water, the stink was not so bad. Ships lay at anchor everywhere, out for three hundred yards into the water, and beyond that was simply blue—no end, no farther shore, in sight.

Alack had never thought to see such a place.

What farther shores lay beyond here—what the Westland would be like, where people were fairer of skin and lighter of eye and worshipped hedonistic gods who were little more than powerful, undisciplined men—he could only begin to imagine.

He found Kol Abaddon standing near the loading plank of a small ship, watching as bundles of cloth, wood, and spices were carried up, wrapped in bundles and covered with waterproofed skins. A single mast and sail in the midst of the ship promised adventure to come.

"This is our ship?" Alack asked, his stomach tightening with excitement at the journey—and greening slightly at the thought of braving the sea with so little to protect them.

Kol Abbadon grunted. He looked surlier than usual—apparently he shared none of Alack's excitement about the journey.

When the captain yelled, "All aboard!", Alack heard Kol Abbadon mutter, "The People of the land were never meant to ride on the sea."

The prophet led the way to a place on the far deck against the rail, in between piles of cargo that were tied down with heavy ropes, and plunked himself down. So much for any hope of a cabin or protection from the elements. Alack sat down uneasily in front of him; there wasn't much room at the rail to squeeze in beside.

"Make sure you can hang onto something," Kol Abaddon said without even a hint of a smile. "Else I'll tie you down to one of these cargo heaps."

"Have you been to sea before?" Alack ventured.

"Once going and once coming. Never wanted to do it again."

This was the most personal feeling Alack had heard from the prophet yet, and he didn't want to give the exchange up too quickly—even if there wasn't much that was positive about it. "Where did you go?" he asked.

But the prophet just answered that with a scathing glance and then turned his head away and stared out toward the waters.

The People were not a seagoing folk. They never had been. The Sacred Land was tucked into the mountains and valleys of the interior world, and they had no reason to take to the dangerous ocean swells.

Others came to them and traded with them; the whole world, it seemed, was drawn to the Holy City. Or they had been, once. Alack knew from his father's stories and the tales of others that long ago, the Holy City had been five times the place of beauty and honour and wealth that it was now. Some blamed the Great God's caprice for the gradual slide. Others said it was judgment; that the Holy People had forgotten the Great God and turned from his ways, and for that reason his favour was removed from them.

Alack supposed his own opinion should be the second, though he hardly knew their history or how to know what the Great God wanted from them. The Holy City was still a great place, wealthy and renowned throughout the world. It was hard to imagine it greater.

Out of nowhere, Kol Abaddon said, "Wealth can be a safeguard, but just as much it can be an invitation to robbers and thieves. When the favour of the Great God is lost to a city, there is everything to fear."

Alack just stared at him, wondering. Could the man read his thoughts all the time, or just now and again?

If Kol Abaddon heard that question, he didn't answer it. The crew was busy casting off; Alack sank further back into the cargo piles to stay out from under their feet. Even under the hot sun the sea air was brisk; he drew his cloak around him and wished he had one to give Kol Abaddon. That had been foolish—not using some of the money to buy the prophet some way to keep warm.

But never mind. When he looked at the prophet again, he saw that the man wore a robe wrapped around his shoulders. Where that had come from, he could not begin to guess.

A week as the prophet's disciple, and Alack felt the man was more a mystery than he had ever been.

Beyond the harbour, the sea was rougher than Alack had imagined. He was soon spray-soaked and sick to his stomach, clinging to the cargo ropes as the ship pitched in the waves. Kol Abaddon said nothing but grew visibly stormier the further they sailed—petulant, in fact. If Alack hadn't been so sick he might have been tempted to laugh.

By midnight the sea had calmed, and they lay on the deck staring up at a clear sky full of stars while the sail filled with a light wind and they flew forward, the captain somehow knowing where to go. Alack marveled at that and at the fact of being here at all.

He was grateful, in the immense strangeness of the whole experience, for Kol Abaddon's company. The man might be a terrible conversationalist and odd by anyone's reckoning, but at least he was familiar. The sailors' voices all spoke in tongues Alack did not recognize; even the smell of the food they ate was strange to him—albeit it was mingled with the scent of the spices in the cargo, the pitch waterproofing the ship and its haul, and the salt air permeating everything.

"Everything evil comes from the sea," Kol Abaddon announced, without warning.

A terrible conversationalist indeed.

"What do you mean?" Alack asked.

"Long ago, when the Great God created the world, all lay under the water. It was formless, chaos. But the Great God spoke and drew the land up from the water, and on the land he created man and marked the boundaries of his dwelling places. He marked the edges of the sea and commanded the waves that they might come thus far and no farther, that chaos might not swallow up the land again."

Alack listened, fascinated. It was a familiar story—and yet not quite familiar. Naam had told him the story of creation since his youth, but this idea of a threat from the sea—this he had not heard.

"There was another world before ours," said Kol Abaddon almost casually.

This Alack had never heard before. He turned his head and tried to see his mentor in the darkness—to no avail.

"Did you never wonder why, in the beginning, everything was under water?"

Alack shook his head, realized Kol Abaddon couldn't see him either, and started to say "No"—but the prophet didn't wait. He continued on.

"Long ago there was a world here, and great races of beings that were beautiful and glorious. But of these, one turned against the Great God and tried to become like him, demanding that creation worship him. His rebellion caught up many others and their hearts and their works turned to great evil, nothing but violence and perversion. Thus the Great God brought judgment upon them by releasing the seas from their bounds, and the old world was swallowed in water and darkness."

"Becoming without form and void," Alack said, repeating the familiar words of the creation story he'd always known.

"Just so. But the rebel did not die, for he was not a man that he should be mortal. All his works were destroyed, but his spirit continued, festering in the waters. That is why the Great God put bounds on the sea, and that is why evil still comes up from it."

"Who was this rebel?" Alack asked.

"Ask not who he was, but who he is. He was once called the Prince of Light, but that is not his name any longer. Now he is called the Serpent, Leviathan the great Sea Monster. And the Dragon."

Alack's eyes fixed on the constellations above. "The Dragon? The same Dragon that is in the stars?"

"The very same," Kol Abaddon said.

The same Dragon Isha ran to embrace. But if the Sacred Land ran to the arms of the sea—

Alack shuddered. Suddenly the dark, menacing world all around

RACHEL STARR THOMSON

him seemed not just a body of water but the whole of reality—swallowed, drowned.

And he and Kol Abaddon alone escaped, riding over the sunken cosmos in a ship.

<hr />

Rechab slipped through the darkness toward the river, following the sound of the water. The night was not a friendly one, the moon mostly gone, the shadows deep. Jackals barked not far away, and she tried not to think of what else she might encounter in the darkness.

She was grateful that she had ceased running so close to the river. It was not until after darkness fell that she realized she could hear the lapping of water. If not for that, venturing out would likely end with her lost and needing to wait till dawn before taking another step.

She had been gone some hours by now. She had heard no sounds of pursuit and could only hope they were searching for her elsewhere—far enough away that she could make good headway up the river before they began to seek her in this direction.

Her mind returned to the mystery of why she was being pursued at all, but with no new information, she was no closer to finding an answer. Flora might be able to help her now—now that Amon had come to Essea, maybe something of the truth had come out. But Flora was still within the community's walls, and Rechab had no way to reach her without betraying her own whereabouts.

Her heart ached dully at having sacrificed a friend. As though leaving home and father and friends and her expected future had not been sacrifice enough, now she was losing the one person who had been any comfort or hope to her. The one person who had promised anything like a future.

Ironic that just that morning she had been chafing at the idea of living in Essea—even of having to stay there temporarily until the threat passed. What else had she imagined herself doing?

Ahead, she could make out the faint glimmer of light on water. The sounds, too, of water over rock, told her she was nearly there. The river was low, in some places barely more than a stream, but it was wide and welcoming in the night. Rechab made her way there carefully, swallowing compulsively as the scent of water met her—though she had slept through the worst heat of the day, she was incredibly thirsty. She knelt in a mostly dry part of the riverbed and felt her way forward to the flowing water, drinking from her cupped hands until her thirst was quenched.

She tried not to imagine anything else drinking at the river at this time of night—other things, most of which could see in the dark far better than she could.

The sound of baaing only a few feet away startled her so badly she nearly screamed. But it was only sheep—a little herd of sheep, now stamping and moving and rushing as one down into the water, muddying it with their hooves. But she didn't mind. She was done drinking for the moment, and their presence made her think of home. And Alack. A pang of loneliness struck again, but in some way the sheep helped abate it too, and so she was glad. She reached out to try to find one and pat it, but nothing came to hand, and she thought better of staying in the riverbed while herds were moving through and backed away, back to the sandy banks with their cutting grasses and murky pools. She wondered who the herd belonged to and if, come daylight, the herdsmen would prove friendly. She feared to let anyone see her, given that Amon would surely be searching for her, but did she truly have any hope of getting away without help? She didn't even have a skin to carry water or any real way to obtain food. She strained her ears for any indication that the shepherd was near, but she heard nothing other than the sheep themselves.

Deciding that as long as she was near the river she didn't need a way to carry water, Rechab determined it would be best to stick to her original plan and get as far upriver as she could under cover of darkness. Other villages and herdsmen would be found along the water, and hopefully she would find someone to aid her. But while she was still within Amon's reach, she could not feel safe—and she certainly had nothing to offer in return for help that would be more tempting to any local people than Amon's money.

A faint, niggling idea came to her at that moment, but she dismissed it as wrong. She would maintain some standard of honesty and self-respect as she fled, no matter what challenges came her way.

The sheep that had charged into the river where she stood were only outliers of a bigger flock; she found herself wandering through groups of them in the darkness. They ignored her, and she felt safe in their midst. Where there were sheep there would also be dogs and shepherds, deterrants to jackals and desert lions and robbers alike. It occurred to her that, perhaps, the Great God whose worship she had dedicated herself to was watching out for her.

Provided she ever got free of her pursuers and found a future, she would take a lamb to the temple and sacrifice to the Great God. It was true enough that the temple had become a haunt of many gods, but originally it had belonged to him, and his priesthood still served there. She didn't know where else she could formally honour him. She didn't know much at all about being a worshipper of the Great God—and that, it seemed to her, was an oversight.

She was one of the Holy People. Their whole identity as a nation was shaped around having been chosen by the Great God and placed in the Sacred Land. So why had she not known that the temple was built according to his own instructions? And why didn't she know much of anything about serving him? He seemed a specific and interested deity, very unlike the frightening gargoyles served by the nations around them. Flora called the idols of other peoples "abominations"; the term felt apt.

In truth, her decision to become a worshipper of the Great God had been an act of desperate self-protection. If she dedicated herself to one deity, another deity would have to relinquish its claims on her—she hoped. And she might have some chance of being supernaturally protected.

She chewed her lip as she walked, keeping the sound of the river to her left and the baaing and rustling of the herds to her right. She wondered if you were supposed to do something ceremonial when you dedicated yourself to the Great God—offer a sacrifice or take a vow. She wished she had asked Flora while she still had a chance. There wasn't much she could do about any of that right now anyway; hopefully the Great God would see her good intentions and she would have time to figure it all out.

Walking in the dark was an agonizingly slow process. The terrain was rocky and uneven, and she had to feel out every footfall to avoid turning an ankle or catching her clothes in a tangle of thorns. But she did not even consider turning back.

It wasn't fear driving her now, it was . . . something else.

A certainty. An inner knowing that she was not wrong to be afraid of what was behind her, nor to be convinced that it was in fact pursuing her.

She stopped, still as death, at the murmur of human voices. Men, somewhere close by.

Shepherds, she decided. She heard no indication of threat or even that they knew she was near. Moving a little farther brought her slightly up a rise, and then she could see a low fire burning some two hundred feet away, and shadows moving around it. Once again loneliness and fear wrestled within her, but fear won out. She had no reason to believe shepherds would be friendly to a woman traveling by herself in the middle of the wilderness at night, and even besides issues of personal safety, she couldn't afford to be delayed.

She would have given anything to have Alack by her side. With the sheep herd all around and the shepherds sitting by their watchfire, she felt close to him—but so far away, at the same time.

He would be pleased, she thought, to know she had given herself to the worship of the Great God. If he truly had gone to apprentice himself to Kol Abaddon, then he had done the same thing.

She smiled. However doomed any romance between them might have been, they would always be kin in heart.

CHAPTER 12

Flora Laurentii the Unlucky had never felt so deserving of her name.

Few of those who knew her story had ever stopped to wonder how she felt about any of it. How she felt was a complex tangle. She had not loved her first husband, who was far older than she and bad tempered, but she had wept when he died nonetheless—because she was only a child, and it was death, and she had never lost anything so profound as a husband before. Her second marriage, seen by most as a conniving grab on her part, was in fact loving; when her second husband died only two weeks after their wedding, she wept for him and for the woman she was becoming. Curse-Slayer, they whispered at the funeral. As though she could not hear them.

From that marriage had come blessings, of course. Wealth and power. And she had handled them well—far, far better than anyone had anticipated. She had, in fact, shocked everyone in her social circles, but she insulated herself from their shock by using her wealth and power to create a world of her own and stay out of theirs. It worked. Not long after that she found the community at Essea and was accepted into their ranks—and she who had long been a private admirer and even worshipper of the Great God became a public religious fanatic. But they accepted her in the community. They allowed her to enter as a stranger and foreigner, to learn and to pray with them, to be fully accepted as the convert she was even though, by the Great God's own laws, she knew she could never set foot in the temple.

To lose them now, to lose that fellowship and acceptance, was worse than the death of two husbands and worse than the shattering of two previous futures.

And on top of all of that, she had lost Rechab. Thrown out of her home for trying to help someone, and now she did not even know where that someone had gone.

She passed through the interior yard at the busiest time of the day, ignoring the clusters of men and women who were coming for bread and water. Ignoring their stares. She knew what she looked like. She'd gone from a furious rage upon seeing Amon in the yard—a rage in which she had turned on both the trader and the Teacher and railed against them with all the force of the injustice she felt—to storming out into the wilderness and searching for Rechab, meanwhile weeping and berating herself and ordering herself to let go of everything she cared about and watch it fall away, because without question it would be lost to her forever when she returned.

When she passed through the gates it was to be informed—by a guard, who came to meet her—that she was expected to appear in the long hall the following morning.

She knew why.

She told him yes and pushed by, doing all within her power to make it to her hut and past the stares without actually exploding.

Above all she was angry at the Great God.

Yes, she knew she was less than the Holy People. Yes, she knew the circumstances of her birth and that she would forever be marked not only a foreigner but also illegitimate, and yes, she knew that the best appellation anyone had ever found for her was "Unlucky." Yes, she knew that was too worldly and too headstrong and too rich.

But didn't he care that her heart had sought after him with single-minded focus from her youth?

Didn't he care that she had given up everything to worship him, to be counted as part of his congregation?

For *this* to happen, now—to be thrown out of the Great God's presence because she was trying to help one of his people escape one of his enemies!

This was so wrong.

So terribly, horribly unjust.

And it hurt. Badly.

Flora the Unlucky had known rejection most of her life, but this was the one rejection she had never wanted to face, never wanted to feel. She knew she was unworthy. She had hoped the Great God would allow her to stay in his presence anyway.

She pushed aside the hanging curtain that served as a door and threw herself down on the floor of the hut, wondering when Rechab had left here and how she had known she was in danger. The memory of praying together taunted her and she knew she could not be at home here again even if the Teacher were to tell her she could stay; even if he loaded her with penance and ordered her to cleanse her soul but promised she would not have to leave if she only did that. She could not stay here while the community had betrayed Rechab, while Rechab was still in danger, and while Amon remained a guest.

That was the worst of it all. Perhaps she could regain everything she loved and cared about if she would repent.

But she could not repent.

Not of this. Not this time.

She wished Kol Abaddon were here.

She stared across the dimly-lit five feet of space from brick wall to brick wall, with its hanging covering the narrow window and its hard-packed earthen floor, and she wished the prophet were here.

To explain this to her.

To speak for the Great God.

In all her life, she had never met someone so full of fire as Kol Abaddon. He had known her as a woman of God, and her heart had leaped at that.

She believed, firmly, that he heard from the Great God and spoke for him. His visions were rumoured all over the Sacred Land and had often been shared within Essea itself; some questioned whether they were truth, and many thought them only true in a metaphysical sense, but she believed them completely.

She remembered, a little bitterly, the offer she had made him. To do anything she could to meet his needs—feed him, house him, pay him for his work. Finance his travels. He hadn't taken her up on any of it—hadn't allowed her that chance to transform filthy lucre into something sacred.

As it was, everything sacred was about to be lost to her, and filthy lucre would be all she had.

Flora the religious fanatic would become Flora the worldly merchantwoman after all, and probably full time.

Unless *she* took up having visions and wandering in the wilderness dressed in camel skins.

Women, even highly religious ones, did not usually do that sort of thing.

She had believed, fervently, that when the judgment of the Great God came to the Sacred Land, she would be safe in Essea. There, where everyone lived to honour and pray to the God, surely calamity would pass them by. How could it be any other way?

But then, how could the community act in a way that was so . . .

"Wrong," she said out loud, liking the weight of the word, the heavy finality of it. Someone had to say it. Even if she had already said it, plenty and plenty loudly, when she lost her temper earlier and told the Teacher he was taking the devil's part.

"That," she had said, pointing at Amon with shaking hand, "is evil and abominable, and you are little better if you will welcome it here!"

She groaned and leaned forward, hugging her middle. There was little hope she could find a way to make this right. If only her mouth was a little less bold, and her heart a little less hot, and the Teacher a little less wrong.

She arose in the darkest part of the night, as usual, for prayer. And this time she almost wished for weights on her hands. She certainly wished for Rechab's presence. Only that things might be turned back, that the clock might reverse, that there might be some other way forward than leaving this place.

But there was none.

She didn't have words to pray that would get past the anger and abandonment she felt, so she sat in the Great God's presence in something between a sulk and a heartbreak until the allotted amount of time was up and she could try, fitfully, to sleep.

Tomorrow they would throw her out and she would not be a sister of the desert anymore. She would be Flora Laurentii Infortunatia, wealthy, powerful, unlucky, and afraid.

She woke up again, in pitch blackness, to the knowledge that someone was in her hut and was positioned over her with a knife.

Her hand shot out and grabbed his wrist as he brought the knife down. He wasn't expecting it, or her strength, and she wrenched his arm aside so the knife plunged into the hard dirt as she sat up and cracked her elbow down on the back of his neck as hard as she could manage.

If he'd hoped for a quiet kill, he'd picked the wrong woman.

"Murder!" she shouted as she threw herself onto the man's back, grabbing him around the neck with one arm and reaching for the knife with the other, all the while trying to use her body weight to keep him down. If she hadn't caught him so off guard, she suspected he'd have killed her already—this was a small man, but his strength seemed greater than his size.

She shouted again, something unintelligible even to herself, as he managed to get onto his knees and slam her back against the brick wall. The wind knocked from her lungs, she fell to her knees and coughed, her eyes still fixed on the shadowy form before her. She darted forward on her knees, avoiding another knife thrust, but this time she lacked both strength and leverage, and nothing about her feint qualified as an attack. His hand closed around her throat. She clawed at it, trying to see where the knife was, twisting and struggling to get free.

Someone burst through the door, and then two someones, and her attacker was hauled away from her. He released her throat as her rescuers grabbed his arms. Supporting herself on her knees with one hand in the dust, she held her throat with her other hand, still heaving and choking for air.

"Are you all right?" One of the desert brothers, a familiar voice. She nodded, not sure if they could see her in the dark, but she couldn't answer yet.

Gentle arms enfolded her shoulders, and a sister's voice spoke. "Come with me. It will be all right."

Rachel Starr Thomson

Twenty minutes later Flora sat in the long hall amidst the light of oil lamps. She had been examined by two of the sisters and proclaimed alive, unstabbed, and relatively undamaged, which she could have told them herself if they had waited for her to get her breath back. She was shaken, however, and angry.

After a ten-minute inspection the Teacher had come, with two of his disciples, and revealed to her the identity of her attacker.

"And yet you still stand by your decision to allow his master entrance here?" she said.

"Amon did not know his servant's whereabouts; he was not behind the attack. We have questioned him."

"For what, five minutes?"

"He is telling the truth," the Teacher insisted.

Flora sulked. Everything hurt—her stomach, her rib cage, her throat, her back where he had slammed her into the wall. She had known, somehow, that it was him—the Hill slave possessed by a daemon, the one who had declared ownership of Rechab.

"The slave is wild and uncontrolled," the Teacher said. "Amon tries to help him, but . . ."

"He is possessed," Flora said. "A daemon of the Hill People controls him. And Amon keeps him in his retinue, though he has displayed this before."

She was not sure whether she was angrier at the Teacher or at herself. She had thought herself successful at casting the daemon out of the man. Had she only been fooling herself?

What real power could she have, after all?

"We will see to it that the man is contained and this cannot happen again," the Teacher said. "We thank the Great God no real damage was done."

"Did you ask him why?" she asked.

The Teacher only stared at her.

"Did you ask him why?" she pressed. "Why did he attack? Why me? Because I helped Rechab? And what claim do they think they have on her?"

"This has nothing to do with her," the Teacher said. "Amon's claims on Rechab are another matter entirely."

"Then this is just coincidence," Flora said. "No, there could be no connection between a trader hunting down an innocent child and his servant attacking the woman who tried to help that child, could there?"

"Flora, you tread on dangerous ground," the Teacher said. He sounded unhappy—not angry so much as frustrated and miserable.

"It has already cost me everything," Flora said. "How much more danger can I dare? Unless you will tell me that in the morning, you do not intend to dismiss me from fellowship."

He sighed deeply. The sound was genuinely pained.

"Flora, I spoke angrily to you this morning, but it gives me no joy to see you leave us. I would far rather you repent."

"But I cannot do that," Flora said. "Because you are in the wrong. You know you are in the wrong."

Her voice broke. She looked up at him, daring to let her heart show. She had trusted this man, followed him, obeyed him, for years. Her voice still breaking, she went on. "This has ever been a place of refuge. A place to worship and to seek the Great God in spirit and in truth, though all the rest of the nation fall away into apostasy and idol worship. What has come over you that you would welcome an enemy of the God and endanger one who is just beginning to seek him? Teacher, I do not understand."

He met her gaze, and she saw heartbreak in his eyes. Her own filled with tears—for him, for herself, for Rechab, for whatever was happening here.

He answered in a voice too low for the others to hear. "Flora, I am not making any decision lightly. There are lives in my hands, and I do not wish to endanger them. But please, believe me—no more did I wish to endanger yours."

She let her tears fall without stopping them. "This is just business, then," she said.

He winced, but he did not answer that.

"I understand," she said. She stood slowly. "I really do."

Somehow, in the space of one conversation, the difference between them had been leveled. There was not so much difference between the Teacher of Essea and Flora the merchantwoman after all.

"I have ordered guards posted around your hut," the Teacher said. "No one will bother you further tonight."

She nodded.

Neither of them would speak of tomorrow.

Before she left the hall, she paused and turned slightly. "The man who attacked me—where is he?"

"Under guard in one of the huts," the Teacher said.

Flora was not sure why she asked, nor was she sure why, upon leaving the hall, she sought out the guarded hut in the gloom of torch-light and went there instead of her own. The guards stepped into her path, questioning.

"I want to see him," she said.

"We can't promise you it's safe," one of the brothers told her.

"Has he been wild? Threatened you?"

The man shook his head. "He's been subdued. But I don't know that he'll stay that way."

"Then come in with me," Flora said. "Offer me your protection. If something goes wrong, you won't be held responsible for it. Everyone here can testify I asked to be let in."

The guards exchanged glances, but she knew she had won. She was not accustomed to playing the woman of influence here—but when she assumed that role, there were few who could withstand her will.

The hut was larger than her own, but the inside was darker, as the roof was more thickly thatched. The walls were rounded and lacked any opening. As she entered, one of the guards handed her a torch.

She lifted it and saw the slave huddled against the far wall. He had been stripped of weapons and his hands and feet bound. But he stared at her without shame or fear. His eyes gleamed in the firelight like an animal's.

Grateful for the guard at her back, Flora lifted the torch a little higher and demanded, "Do you know who I am?"

"Yes," the slave said. His voice was thick with the accent of the Hill People—her mother's people. The sound was more than familiar. He might have been her own brother or cousin, she thought—she would have no way to know.

"Tell me why you attacked me," she said.

He answered nothing.

Clearing her throat, she lifted the torch a little higher again and said, "Tell me why you followed us here. What is your claim on Rechab?"

"She belongs to us," he hissed. "She is sold to us."

"Sold by whom? To whom? Not to Amon."

"No," the slave said. "To *us*. To Kimash."

The name sent shivers down her spine, and she closed her eyes for a split second.

Kimash, abomination of the Hill People. The fear that had driven her into the arms of the Great God as a child.

How ironic that one of his servants should try to slay her, here, in the shelter of the Great God's community, so many years after she had run.

In the torchlight, for the first time she noticed dark markings on the back of his hands, and she thought she saw them on the back of his neck also. They too were familiar. A man so marked was given to the service of Kimash—he was a temple slave.

How he had come to be in Amon's retinue she could not begin to guess.

"Who sold Rechab to you?" she asked again.

"One whose authority you cannot gainsay," the slave—or the beast living within him—said. "Her own father."

He cackled with laughter. She pressed on.

"Why does Amon follow us? What is his part in all of this?"

But the slave only looked up at her and laughed.

Frustrated, she turned to go.

But she had one last question.

"Rechab—" she said. "If Rechab comes to your master, what will happen to her?"

The slave grinned garishly in the light. "Kimash will eat her flesh and her bones," he said.

Flora gritted her teeth and left the hut.

"Do you wish accompaniment back to your hut?" the guard asked her.

"No," she told him. "I am not going there. I am leaving."

"But—"

"Why wait one more night?" she asked, sorry to take out her emotions on him but unable to hold herself back. "I think my friend is in terrible danger, and Flora the desert fanatic is no help to her. The Teacher will order me to leave in the morning as it is. I may as well go and spare him the trouble. Spare all of us the trouble."

The guard's expression changed. He had been here as long as she— and while there was little real friendship between the men and women of Essea, yet she counted him among those she trusted and cared for. From the look in his eyes, he felt the same.

If many more would give her that look, it might almost convince her to repent her position and stay. Yes, leaving tonight was right. She could give herself no room to turn away from what she knew she had to do.

"You have been one of us," he said. "You will always be one of us."

"And if the Teacher proclaims me cut off?" she said.

"But he will not," the guard said. "For if you are leaving, there is no cause to dismiss you."

She smiled. "Thank you for that."

"Surely there is another way . . ."

"There is not. But if you would tell the Teacher what you said tonight, I would be grateful. And tell him what you heard the slave say. And tell him . . ." She paused to think her words through. "Tell him that I do understand, but I know, also, that what seems necessary may prove to be a poor move after all. In that case, it is always best to cut one's losses and do all in one's power to move in a new direction, rather than pushing a bad decision to its inevitable end. It is a wise saying. Will you remember that?"

"I will," the guard said.

———•◆•———

Dawn brought heat with it.

Rechab was glad to be near the river still. She had passed through the last of the herd in the night, and the first light of day found her still walking, now through the cool of the riverbed itself. It was not the safest place to be—she was too easy to spot, and too vulnerable to predators that might be at the water to drink—but she had grown wearied in the night and feared that in her state of exhaustion, she would lose the river. Better to walk along the inside of its banks than to wander into the trackless desert and be completely lost.

She thanked the Great God that she still had her life.

Through the light of the rising sun she could make out the smudge of a village on the riverbank, not far now. With a night's walking behind her, plus the hours from the day before, she judged it finally safe to stop and seek some kind of aid. At least Amon would not have been here already; if he came behind, asking for her, she hoped the villagers would not take his part. In any case, she would keep out of sight as much as possible and deal only with those she had to deal with. She wanted to occasion as little speculation as she could.

The village itself was unremarkable. Built on the banks of the river, its houses were made of mud bricks and reeds; she guessed that no more than twelve families resided here. Fields of corn stretched out on three sides; women and field workers were already tending the crop, which had grown no higher than her knees. She let her hand graze the tops of the corn as she approached. This was a bad place to remain inconspicuous. Perhaps, after all, she would have to rely on their discretion to keep her way secret. The chances that she could get in and out without everyone in the village knowing it were slim to none.

As she drew near the cluster of mud brick houses, her eyes fell on a tall, dark structure in the middle of the village.

A shrine. And not to the Great God.

She had seen its like in the Holy City, though on a far grander scale. This was one of the gods of the South, a god of rivers and of harvests. Only natural that these people should seek its favour—except that these were Holy People.

In the Holy City the sight of the many shrines and grottos and high places dedicated to the gods of the nations had possessed her with uncontrollable, unreasonable fear. But here and now, a very different sense filled her. A sense of indignation against a people that would leave their own roots and seek after strange idols, and a sense of being different—of being set apart.

Of being holy.

This, she had never felt before.

Had the Great God's eyes, fixed upon her in the long hall of Essea, marked her somehow?

She didn't realize she was standing in the middle of the street, staring at the thing, until a voice behind her said, "And will you be needing something, Stranger?"

She turned, her heart pounding. An old woman was staring up at her, two parts inquiring and one part amused.

"Are you needing to inquire of the god Aneth?" she asked, motion-

RACHEL STARR THOMSON

ing toward the shrine. "Or is it only water and food you're seeking?"

"Water and food," Rechab asked, grateful for the woman's giving her words. "And . . . and some direction."

"Lost, are you?" the woman asked.

"I am following the river," Rechab said.

The old woman nodded as though she understood what that meant. "And where do you come from?"

"I . . ." She hesitated. She had no idea what to say. Should she identify herself as being from Bethabara—what seemed an immeasurable distance away? Or did she tell the woman she had been in the desert, with the community of Essea? Would that be saying too much?

"If you don't know where you come from," the woman said, "I don't blame you for not knowing where you're going. But come, follow me. I can give you something to eat and drink."

"Thank you," Rechab stuttered. The old woman had already turned and was ambling toward the far end of the village. Rechab followed. "May I know your name?" she asked.

"Zeruh," the old woman said. "Grandmother to half this village and scourge to the rest of them. Especially to them that worship Aneth. I am an old woman; I have no time for interloping deities that neither my fathers nor their fathers knew."

Rechab paused an instant in following the woman. "Are you a worshiper of the Great God, then?"

"Sooner the Great God than these foreign things, but as long as corn grows and the water doesn't dry up, I'm happy." The old woman stopped and gave her a sharp eye. "Just enough religion to keep your soul peaceful and your stomach fed, that's all anyone needs. You come up from the desert hideaway downriver? The community of fanatics?"

Rechab blushed. "I . . . I passed through there."

"Best not take up with their ideas. Does nothing but cause misery and trouble. Spend your life in dryness and dust, is all they do."

"They say they give up everything in order to gain everything," Rechab said, remembering what Flora had told her when they first approached Essea.

The old woman snorted. "Seems to me they forgot to get around to the gaining."

Rechab followed the old woman to the door of one of the mud brick huts, where she was left on the doorstep as the woman gathered food—a skin of wine, sacks of flat bread, dried figs, dates, and fish. Rechab's mouth watered as she waited, her stomach churning at the sight and smell of food. She had walked a long way on little sustenance—the fare at Essea was not rich at the best of times, she suspected—and her body reminded her of it now.

The old woman waved her back away from the door as she emerged bearing the sacks and the wineskin—and then, to Rechab's surprise, she found herself facing an extended hand. The food and drink had been dropped, and the woman was waiting for payment.

"Oh," Rechab said, flustered. Of course she should not have assumed it was a gift—but the woman had seemed as though she wanted to help.

To make matters more embarrassing, several villagers had gathered around while Rechab was waiting. Clearly they had spotted her for a stranger and come in from the fields.

"I ask no more than market value," the old woman said. "Two shekels and I'll hold my peace."

"I'm afraid I have nothing," Rechab stammered. "I thought . . . I'm sorry. I have nothing."

"On credit, then," the woman said. "But I'll require something as surety."

The newcomers were making noises, none of them encouraging. Rechab felt suddenly cornered and realized she was being swindled. The price the woman had asked was sinking in, and she knew it was too high—much too high.

"On credit," she said slowly, "one half-shekel, but I have nothing to leave with you other than my word."

The woman motioned toward her feet. "Your sandals are good."

"I can't give you those!" Rechab burst out. "I've a long way to go!"

"That's not my problem, is it?" the woman asked. Her eyes narrowed. "Now, are you going to find a way to pay me, or am I going to charge you with trying to rob me?"

Rechab's heart sank. Of course that threat was nonsense—she had not even touched the provisions the woman had gathered for her, unasked. But she suspected the judges had already gathered around, and she would find no friendship here.

The old woman was looking her over with an eye that made Rechab's skin crawl. "We can find ways to make you pay," she said. "You'd make a good field worker. Or something else."

The idea that had come to mind in the night, the one Rechab had dismissed as dishonest, came back to her as the only possible option—the only thing that might stop these people from making a slave of her here and now.

She straightened her shoulders and steadied her voice, adopting the tone she had used as a manager first of her father's affairs and then of Flora's.

"You would not dare," she said. "All right, I will take the provisions on credit. They can be laid to the account of Flora Laurentii."

The woman's eyes widened, and she heard the flurry of whispers from the growing crowd of villagers.

"You're bluffing," the woman said. "You have no rights to the wealth of Flora Laurentii."

Rechab looked her in the eye. "You force me to reveal myself when I would have rather stayed unknown," she said. "But I am Flora's business manager. Lay a hand on me and you will pay for it with more than shekels."

The crowd shrank back, and Rechab had to catch herself to keep from sighing with relief. It would work. Flora's money was power—even here.

The old woman's voice was a little shakier now. "And what can you give me for surety?" she said.

"I can give you a note with my own signature," Rechab said.

That occasioned more whispering and fear. Unless she missed her guess, no one here could read or write.

The old woman jerked her head, and a boy went scampering after something—he returned moments later with a reasonably flat piece of sandstone and a sharp tool. Rechab hadn't intended to chisel the note, but she wasn't surprised there was no paper in the village. She took the tools as regally as she could and set to work carving her initials, with the amount owed—one-half shekel. If the old woman could understand the characters, she did not let on. She had gone a little pale. Rechab hoped she was reviewing the possible consequences of mistreating someone of such import in her mind.

"Will you require anything else, Mistress?" a young man asked.

And now that it came down to it—yes, she did. She hadn't meant to open this particular answer or make use of it; she was stealing from Flora and she knew it. But then, would Flora truly object? And what other choice did she have?

"Four things," she said. "I want a mule, saddled. Four more wineskins to add to this one—someone must have more to sell me. A runner to take a message for me. And your silence."

She reviewed all their faces and decided they were properly cowed. Now she could only hope Flora's money and power were more convincing than Amon's. "I have reason to believe I am being followed," she said. "Should anyone come looking for me, you have never seen me. If I find that you have betrayed me, the money I owe you will never reach this village. You can understand that, I trust?"

They nodded and bowed their hands in a pleasing show of submission. The young man who had asked whether anything more was needed stepped forward. "You asked for a runner?" he said.

"I want one of my employees summoned to join me," Rechab said. "One who lives in the village on the other side of Essea. He is called Aaron, the mule driver. I want him told to join me at the head of the river, with a fresh mule and writing materials and arms. Can you give him that message?"

"I can," the young man said. "I know Aaron. I've seen him at market hereabouts."

"Good, good," Rechab said, once again trying not to let the depth of her relief show. She couldn't send word straight to Flora as long as she did not know what had happened in Essea, but Aaron might give her a chance at communicating—or at least of learning what was going on. And if he could bring her a good mule and something with which to write, she could pull off a much more convincing role as Flora's second in command.

Dishonest it might be, but she didn't feel she had much choice.

As various villagers scurried away to do her bidding and others lingered nearby, partly in awe and partly perhaps to keep an eye on her, Rechab concentrated on maintaining a dignified air and disdained to make eye contact with the old woman again. She could feel her presence, lurking nearby, but thought it best to make her displeasure with the woman's conniving and threats clear. Inwardly she shuddered at how willing this woman had been to rob her blind, and then to hand her over to injustice and slavery. The People had laws to prevent such things—laws that tradition said had been given to them by the Great God himself. She knew they were rarely enforced anymore. But never having been a stranger or unprotected before, she had never really faced the reality of that injustice. Her father had often said that Mammon was the only god the People truly worshipped, or, for that matter, any people on the face of the earth. Talk of a Creator and a Lawgiver was all well and good, but Money was the only one true and universal god to hold sway in the daily lives of men and women alike.

That she herself was employing the power of Mammon to get her out of this situation did not escape her, nor did the fact that from here on out, she intended to make her way through the world as the emissary of one of the wealthiest women in the Sacred Land. Yet it was the Great God she would worship, and the Great God she would run to. That decision was made. No matter where she went, she would find a way to learn more about the god to whom she'd sworn fealty, to sacrifice to his honour in the Holy City—no matter how much she hated it there—and to serve him properly.

Not even wealth would stop her in that pursuit. After all, if Flora could do it, so could she.

RACHEL STARR THOMSON

CHAPTER 13

K ol Abaddon slept nearly all of the time for the first three days of the journey. Alack was surprised by this for two reasons: first that he had nearly managed to convince himself, after the many waking nights in the desert, that Kol Abaddon simply never did sleep; and second that for the life of him, he could not understand how anyone could sleep under these conditions. How was it that a man who did not sleep under the desert sky, with a firm earth beneath his feet and the warmth of a fire to comfort him, could snore a perpetual three days with the sea pitching beneath him and the spray making everything cold, wet, and miserable?

Alack himself had decided that once they got home again, he would never, ever again board a ship. If the Great God sent him to some faraway place, he would go overland and take his chances with anything the earth could throw at him.

That was assuming the Great God had not forgotten about him. After the initial rush of visions and nighttime experiences, it was as though everything had gone silent. Nothing, no communication, no vision. He fretted and wondered if this silence was normal, but the only person he could ask was asleep.

The sailors ignored them both completely, in fact giving them a wide berth. Alack rationed out their supply of food in meagre amounts and passed his time counting down the hours until he could try to eat again. At least his stomach had settled down after the initial casting away.

It would be hours before he ate again. Night was thick over the water now, and only a lone watchman on the deck was still awake. Alack sat with his back against the rail, wrapped in his cloak, absently watching the watchman and the bobbing oil light next to him. A brisk wind had them moving over the water, and the ship rolled and pitched as always.

He was thinking of Kol Abaddon's story about the Dragon that lost its world to the flood and then rose up again from the depths to trouble this one. The clear sky overhead displayed the Dragon in all its glory, and Isha, rushing toward it.

Tonight his heart ached as he looked at her. Ached for home. Ached for his father, even for the dumb sheep. Ached for Rechab.

Especially for Rechab.

As he gazed at the sky, he thought it was Rechab he could see rushing to the Dragon's embrace.

He shuddered.

Someone came up from below and switched places with the night watchman, exchanging words in a language Alack couldn't understand. Both men looked over at him; he saw their glances but tried to ignore them, uncomfortable. Why were they staring?

It took him a moment to realize Kol Abaddon was awake, and standing.

He wasn't sure the prophet had stood even once since boarding the ship. But now he was standing with one hand on the cargo ropes, leaning out over the dark water with every muscle tense.

The prophet was listening, and Alack could feel the tension of his listening, and he thought the watchmen could feel it too.

He opened his mouth to ask a question, but Kol Abaddon's hand rose to silence him.

The prophet's eyes stayed fixed on the water.

And then he turned, and his expression was wild—mad.

Alack was not sure he had ever seen him like that.

He pointed to the water and raised his voice to what was almost a shriek. "There is something in the water!"

Alack scrambled to his feet, embarrassed, and tried to reach out for the prophet as he would if his father had stumbled and he needed to help him. To calm him down. Kol Abaddon brushed him aside and raised his voice even louder. "Wake the men! There is something in the water! Change the sail and get us away from here!"

One of the watchmen called back in the language of the People, his accent thick. "There is nothing. Go back to sleep. You dream."

"A dragon," the prophet said. "There is a dragon in the waters. Leviathan will swallow us whole!"

This time Alack was determined to calm the man down and make him sit, but when he moved to his side, his eye caught sight of something moving on the port side of the ship.

Something breaking the water—cresting.

It was so dark, and so large, that he might have mistaken it for a current or a wave if Kol Abaddon had not already said the word dragon.

As it was, he put both hands on the rails and leaned over, eyes wide, searching for another look to convince himself that he wasn't just seeing things.

But there it was again. Perhaps a hundred yards out. Cresting the waves, bigger than a whale, a humped, scaled darkness like the coil of a serpent.

He licked his lips. "Dragon," he said. He pointed, raised his voice. "Look! It's there!"

The sailors were at his side a moment later, lifting the oil lamp and searching the waters to see what he had seen. The serpent did not disappoint. The unmistakable sight crested again, and this time the sailors swore in their language, and one disappeared belowdecks. Calling all hands.

Alack stood with his feet frozen to the deck. He had seen it crest three times and knew it was getting closer.

Kol Abaddon grabbed his arm in a vice grip. His eyes were still wild, but he had said nothing since his warning to the sailors.

"What is it?" Alack asked.

"It is very darkness," Kol Abaddon answered. "Did I not say all evil comes up from the sea?"

Feet pounded up the stairs and then across the deck and the men were all there, working in the dark, expertly unwinding ropes and changing the sails. Oil lamps lit and the shadows turned to silhouettes. A few orders were given and grunts heard, but for the most part the men worked in silence, as though they feared the dragon would hear.

Alack had never felt so useless or in the way. He could only trust to these strangers to get the boat away, out of the creature's presence. There was nothing he could do.

The sail changed, the boat seemed to pick up speed as it changed direction and skipped over the waves to the east—closer inland. Alack felt a swell of relief and victory as they put the creature behind them—

Until he saw it again, cresting much closer this time.

Shouts told him others had seen it too. His eyes riveted on the water. Somehow his inability to see the whole of the thing made it worse—like the fear that comes in a nightmare when the monster is about to be revealed but has never actually been seen.

And then suddenly there was Kol Abaddon's hand on his shoulder. Just heavy, resting there, like a father's hand. Like Kol Abaddon had never been toward him. And in that hand was comfort and strength and awareness that he wasn't alone.

That if this monster came and capsized their ship, if he drowned in these black waves, he would not do it unknown or unfriended.

But that was the last time they saw the creature that night.

When morning came the ship was running in sight of land, and the sailors were keeping a wary eye on the coast. A reef out to sea hemmed them in close to the shore.

Kol Abaddon had not gone back to sleep, but sat with his back against the rail and his shoulders bare to the sun—a hot sun, hotter here than it had been further out at sea.

"Why are they uneasy?" Alack asked, inclining his head toward the sailors.

"Because the sea is the haunt of monsters, but the shore is the haunt of men. And here, many are pirates. Leviathan has left us no choice but to sail where it is dangerous to sail."

Alack cast a new glance at the shore, transformed suddenly from shelter to menace. "Is the danger real?"

"Of course it is."

"Did the monster really drive us here? Or was it just a dumb creature—just an oversized jackal?"

"Ask the men how many oversized jackals they have seen in their years at sea."

Alack made a face. "I cannot speak their language."

"The answer is I don't know. But sea monsters are more stuff of legend than stuff of reality, except when you are walking with one foot in this world and one foot in the spirit."

Alack turned that one over in his mind. "Are you saying the creature—the leviathan—was something like my visions in the desert? Only we all saw it?"

"Perhaps I am saying it was a portent. A sign to us all that death is coming from the sea."

There was a strain in Kol Abaddon's face that gave weight to a growing conviction in Alack's heart. And perhaps it was the circumstances—all the danger, and the tension and relief and more danger—or perhaps he was just growing more accustomed to his mentor and was tired of knowing so little about him. But whatever the reason, he finally voiced his thoughts.

"Something terrible happened to you at sea, didn't it? You lost someone."

Kol Abaddon looked away. "I was another man then," he said. "That was another life."

"With a sad ending."

"I had a wife and children. Two children. They all three drowned. Does that answer your question well enough?"

No, Alack thought, no, it doesn't. But he didn't know how to answer, and he didn't want to push. This was not a wound to poke at.

"Why did you become a holy man?" he asked instead.

Kol Abaddon stayed silent for some time. Then he said, "Questions drive a man to seek answers. And injustice drives him to seek revenge."

Revenge.

All this time Alack had thought the prophet's warnings were for the sake of trying to save the Sacred Land and its people. But now he thought that was wrong. Now he thought the prophet gave his warnings because he wanted the judgment to come. Because the judgment would be his vengeance.

Once again he wondered what message the wild man of the desert had for the king of the Westland, and how they would deliver it, and what it would all mean.

He could not join his mentor in a desire to see judgment come. For him, the Sacred Land was his father and Rechab and the people of Bethabara and countless nights and mornings and long days tending sheep in the familiar valleys and riverbeds and mountains. It was home. They were home. He wanted to save it, and them.

But he didn't know if that was possible.

A shout drew his attention. He jumped to his feet, steadying himself on the cargo pile, and scanned the shoreline to see what was causing a stir.

He saw it even as some of the other sailors shouted in response, and they were back at work on the sails—picking up speed.

Three long, low boats, narrow and driven by oarsmen, had launched into the water and were moving toward them.

"Pirates?" he asked Kol Abaddon.

The prophet did not answer. Just stared.

One of the boats struck out ahead of them, cutting off the path straight ahead. The other two were between them and the shore, moving toward them at a rapid clip. Faster than it seemed men at oars should be able to move a ship, and yet they were coming.

Alack could see grim expressions on the faces of the sailors. They were pulling out cutlasses and fishing spears. A spear was thrust into his own hands.

"Why don't we go out to sea?" he asked.

"The way is blocked," Kol Abaddon said. "A reef. The pirates know this stretch well."

Perhaps the monster would be the death of them after all.

Kol Abaddon strode forward for a better view, then glanced back at Alack. "Put that spear down," he said.

"But the men gave it to me."

"Put it down. You can't fight. So don't look like a threat. You want the first man to board this ship to run you through?"

But something about the way the prophet said it made Alack think that Kol Abaddon didn't expect the battle to go that way at all. That he expected something no one else did—

Shaking, he put the spear down.

One man on the ship had a bow, and he put arrow to string and fired at the closest attacker. If he hit anyone, there was no sign. The long boat drew closer, and suddenly hooks were shooting out from it and clinging to the cargo ship. Alack swallowed hard as the men rushed to disengage the hooks, but they had dug deep into the wood, and there were already men scaling them.

In a matter of seconds the deck was swarming with pirates. Dark men—skin brown to begin with and blackened by the sun. Eyes fierce. Their arms and faces were tattoed, and they wore skins or stood mostly naked. Rings and wooden plugs adorned their ears, and many of them wore necklaces of teeth or skulls.

One man, whom Alack saw coming over the rail and then straightening on deck, wore a human skull on a rope about his neck.

He swallowed hard. Kol Abaddon had been right. If he had held onto the spear, he would have dropped it by now in sheer terror.

The battle should have been fierce. Barbarian pirates, ruthless and well-armed, against experienced sailors desperate for their lives.

But there was no battle.

Because there was Kol Abaddon.

Even as the barbarians poured onto the ship, the prophet raised both his arms and said something no one could quite make out. And then he said in merchant pidgin, "They are blind, they are blind, take them captive! They cannot see you!"

Confused cries of terror, accompanied by stumbling and flailing, confirmed his words.

The barbarians could not see.

With a shout, the sailors rushed to press their advantage. In minutes they had disarmed the men and herded them into tight circles, surrounded.

Following Kol Abaddon's lead, one of the sailors cried in merchant pidgin, "What do we do with them?"

"Throw them overboard," another said, with a lot of other suggestions in the usual language Alack could not understand. But the tone was unmistakable.

"No," Kol Abaddon said, and his voice froze them all. He strode forward, middeck, his voice and posture and eyes commanding authority.

"You will not kill these men," he said. "They are captives. You will take them home and collect a ransom for their lives, and you will leave here richer men than you dreamed of being when you set out on this voyage."

The suggestion set off a volley of discussion and argument, most of which Alack couldn't follow. But Kol Abaddon cut into the confusion again.

"Kill these men and you will have blood on your hands. They are helpless before you. Their kinsmen dwell all through these coasts; they will pursue you and overtake you and slay you all. Do you think the Great God will show you such favour twice? Do as I say, and all will go well for you. Wash this opportunity away in blood, and all that will come of it is more blood."

The men fell silent at this, and into the quiet came the pleading of the captives—not a word of it understandable to any of them, but the tone unmistakable. These were not like captives taken in battle, bested by superior might. They had not stood a chance.

The captain gave orders. The sales were set, and the ship turned inland. The sailors took it not much farther before dropping anchor; the barbarian attack boats, still attached to the ship by hooks and lines, would serve as skiffs to get them all the way to shore.

Alack stood astonished as all of this transpired. But he was even more astonished when, as the boats began to be loaded, Kol Abaddon motioned for him to line up with the men who were descending the sides of the ship.

"Me?" he asked.

"Of course," Kol Abaddon said. "Why not you?"

Alack had no good reason.

He lined up with the others and made the slippery, frightening journey down the rope to the long boat. It rocked hard underfoot as he landed, and he gripped the sides. But land—oh blessed land would be under his feet in minutes.

The captives were all hustled into the centre of the long boat and tied together, bound hand and foot and neck, before being forced to take up oars and begin rowing. They obeyed, fumbling and clearly terrified. The sailors kept their weapons drawn and did a fair amount of cuffing and poking at the prisoners. Alack didn't like it, but the barbarians cut such a horrific figure of violent thievery that he could not blame the sailors for trying to keep them cowed. Even blind, if they were to get their courage back, Alack feared what they might be capable of.

Kol Abaddon, seated at the helm, did not seem concerned. He looked toward the shore like a man glimpsing new life and drank deeply of the air.

They landed the boats by ramming them up as far as they could onto the sandy beach, and keeping a sharp eye out for any welcoming party, a handful of the sailors jumped out and grabbed the boats to pull them even farther up. Then they unloaded their prisoners, with a good amount of cursing and threats. Kol Abaddon himself took the lead almost immediately, calling for the men to follow him and trekking off into the thick mass of forest that was the landscape here. Alack hurried to keep up.

Almost immediately, what Alack had thought was impenetrable foliage gave way to a wide path hidden just beyond the treeline. Kol Abaddon started down it as though he had always known it was there and as though he knew exactly where it led. All of which, Alack was quite sure, was not true. There was much about his master's history he did not know, but this place was surely not a part of it. Nevertheless, Kol Abaddon's confidence was contagious, and Alack found that if he just stuck very close behind him, his quickly swelling waves of doubt stayed at bay.

Birds called and chattered overhead as they marched through the green terrain. Vines sprawled over the ground and climbed up the trunks of trees and twisted around their branches, some of them flowering, others appearing to choke the lives out of their hosts. The green was overwhelming, but Alack did not like the way the trees hid the sky and the vines hid the trees. Everything felt close and constricted—full of life, yes, but choking and drowning itself in that life. Grateful though he was for solid ground beneath his feet, he felt a fresh ache for the desert sky and the wide horizons of home.

Some of the barbarians began to cry out as they marched, cries not of fear but of joy—recognizing, perhaps, the terrain beneath their feet. The sailors hit them in the backs of their heads and barked for them to be quiet. They were making enough noise as it was.

Alack wondered what sort of greeting awaited them. If they would meet with a village council and negotiate the return of the captives, or if a whole new raiding party would greet them with swords and spears.

He wondered what Kol Abaddon would do then. If he could strike a new enemy blind as well.

The trees thinned and then ceased entirely as they marched into a man-made clearing. Crops grew along the edges, and in the midst the village sat: a collection of thatched huts built of branches and palm leaves and mud.

There was not a human being in sight.

Grumbling arose from the sailors. "You said we would take a ransom," the captain said to Kol Abaddon. "There is no one here to pay!"

"Peace," Kol Abaddon said. "They will come. March on. You will see."

Alack wondered just as much as the men did. What was the prophet thinking? They would enter the very centre of the village and then be attacked by warriors in hiding, waiting to ambush them. Or there was truly no one here, and they would have to find some way of disposing of the captives that would please all of the sailors enough to stop them from engaging in a massacre.

In the centre of the village was a large firepit, still smoking, its embers bright. This, Alack guessed, was the centre of community life.

"Sit the captives around the fire," Kol Abaddon commanded.

The men expressed their surprise and consternation, but the captain reiterated the order. "Do it!"

Still murmuring, the sailors released enough of the captives from their common bonds to seat them around the fire. Soon the barbarians surrounded it, looking for all the world like a village council—but one that was both blinded and bound.

"Now release them," Kol Abaddon said.

Even Alack felt a jolt of shock at that. He couldn't be serious! The sailors looked askance at the prophet and then at their captain, no one moving to obey.

The captain swore—Alack didn't need to understand the words to know the tone—and threw down his cap. Kol Abaddon remained unmoved and expectant.

Finally, swearing again, the captain pulled out a knife and cut the first barbarian loose.

His men followed suit—in action and attitude. They moved despairingly, like men who expected the rope they were hanging to twist around their own necks. Alack wondered why they obeyed at all, and then remembered that Kol Abaddon had, after all, struck the invaders blind. To these men, he didn't look any less dangerous than the tribesmen. At least if it came to a fight, they knew how to battle flesh and blood.

"Step back," Kol Abaddon said when they had finished, and the men obeyed. Then the prophet raised his hands and said, "Now *see*."

The barbarians blinked. Looked around, eyes widening. And then shouted and leaped to their feet. Alack instinctively reached for a weapon and realized he didn't have one—not so much as a shepherd's crook.

But the tribesmen were not attacking. Instead, they turned, forming a wary circle, and eyed Kol Abaddon and the ship's captain. They crouched away, deferent. One of them, the tall man wearing a human skull, stepped forward and bowed at the waist to Kol Abaddon.

Alack, who was standing right next to his mentor, hardly knew what to do.

The barbarian straightened and said something in his language. No one answered. Trying again, he spoke in the familiar market pidgin Alack had heard from traders of all nations—though his was heavily accented.

"You have spared us, Man of Great Power," the man said. "You are welcome in this place."

"You owe us more than a welcome!" the ship captain burst out, angry. "We ought to—"

He cut off his own words as he became aware of what his men had already seen—what Alack had just noticed.

They were not alone in the village after all.

Out of the huts, and out of the jungle beyond them, women and children were gathering into the clearing. They stared wide-eyed at their husbands and fathers, and at the enemy surrounding them.

"The Great God has given you back to your families," Kol Abaddon said, speaking loudly enough for everyone to hear—including those still lurking in the trees.

CHAPTER 14

That night they slept in a grass-thatched hut in the village. Alack relished the dry air and the dry ground and the dry animal skins covering him. He relished the way the ground beneath him stayed still, and the earthy smells that filled his nose instead of salt and pitch and fish. The knowledge that they would soon return to the ship made him all the more grateful for the brief respite—although the air here was more humid than he was accustomed to and the smells and sounds of the forest very different from home.

He knew Kol Abaddon was awake. He had spent enough time listening to the man sleep in the past week at sea to tell the difference in his breathing. He couldn't sleep—and didn't want to, yet, while he was enjoying being on the ground—so he asked instead, "Why did you do it?"

Kol Abaddon grunted questioningly.

"Why did you let the men go free?"

"Serving the Great God is not all judgment," Kol Abaddon said. "Sometimes it is mercy."

Alack thought about that. "Mercy on their families?"

"On us all. We might have killed twenty enemies. Instead we have gained twenty friends."

Alack smiled in the dark. It was true. He had not considered that. "But when you struck the men with blindness, they were terrified." He rolled over and raised himself on his elbows. "It cannot have felt like mercy to them."

"Only because they did not know what the end would be. But they would not have chosen this. They would have chosen to plunder us, and some of them would have died. Men are driven to their own destruction."

Alack ventured the question that had been bothering him since the day he first heard Kol Abaddon proclaiming doom and destruction upon the Holy City—the question he had tried to ask before and received no answer to. "Will the Great God show the People mercy?" he asked.

"No," Kol Abaddon said. His tone brooked no disagreement.

"But why?" Alack asked.

"They do not deserve it," Kol Abaddon said. "Evil has swallowed the People. They are seduced by the Dragon and they walk in his ways. The Great God must destroy them."

Alack lay back down and stared up at the grass thatching, but his mind was in the wadi in the desert: seeing a lamb, seeing Rechab. Feeling a driving desire to save them.

Why had the Great God showed him that? What did it mean? The God had blinded a tribe of marauders in order to have mercy on them. Could there truly be no way to bring about mercy on the People?

"Why do you warn them, then?" Alack asked. "Why try?"

"To make the sentence even more inarguable," Kol Abaddon said. "To make justice clear, for they would not listen when they were given the chance."

Aurelius Florus Laurentinus was not entirely prepared for Nadab the Trader to appear at his door demanding to know where his daughter was.

The big merchant was in a rage, his face flushed red and his enormous shoulders quivering. "Where is she?" he bellowed.

Aurelius kept his voice calm and diplomatic, his whole manner ingratiating. "My friend, I do not know. Is there a reason you think I should know where Rechab is?"

"Because she was last seen here," Nadab said, exploding. "Because she was here in the employ of your sister, in your house, and no one has seen her since that woman left."

Inwardly, Aurelius cursed. He should have known the trouble Flora would bring him had not ended with her departure. He had been dealing with unhappy arrivals for the last weeks, as those with whom she had planned to meet reached his house only to find that their contact had already departed. For the most part, this had worked out in his favour. What they cost him in food, lodging, and entertainment, they would make up for in alliances and contacts. Marah had been exactly right in her advice. But Nadab was another story. And Aurelius did not like being blindsided. He had not known Rechab had gone with Flora.

But then, maybe she hadn't. Or maybe, at least, he could convince Nadab that she hadn't.

"Will you come and take a seat?" Aurelius asked.

"No!" Nadab roared. "You will tell me where my daughter has gone!"

"As I told you, I do not know. But I think you may be mistaken in your assumption—"

"She was last seen when Flora left."

"She may have used Flora's going as a cover."

Nadab narrowed his eyes. "What are you trying to tell me?"

"The shepherd boy, Alack, is also gone. If I am not mistaken, he has not been seen for about the same length of time your daughter has been missing."

Nadab was clearly taken aback. His visage changed as he considered the suggestion. "The little backstabber," he said.

"I take it you think there may be some truth in what I say?"

"The boy came to me before I left for the Holy City, requesting my daughter's hand—or something like that. I was impressed by his spirit and offered him a position with me, which he did not take. He told me he was going out to join the prophet—that he had become a prophet in his own right."

He barked a short laugh. "A prophet—a swindler."

"Aren't all the prophets swindlers?" Aurelius asked, wondering whether he dared to chuckle. He decided not. "Frightening and manipulating the people to their hurt. Nothing more."

"Curse the little scoundrel!" Nadab thundered. "I'll see him flayed alive for this."

Aurelius raised an eyebrow. Such punishment was decidedly out of Nadab's jurisdiction, but men of means lived by their own laws and had their ways of enacting them. Everyone knew this, Aurelius most of all. Favour in the courts had always meant a balancing act between pleasing the king and pleasing the rich men. In recent years, that balance had tipped in the direction of the merchants—hence the wisdom in Marah's advice that he should court the favour of those Flora brought into his circle. The king in Shalem was little more than a trader's puppet—he feasted on tribute they paid him, but the tribute was little more than a bribe. And he kept his own side of the bargain.

Looking the other way, for example, when the merchantmen made their enemies disappear.

Nadab eyed Aurelius with a sudden note of caution, perhaps aware that he had spoken out of turn. But Aurelius simply nodded. He would rather have Nadab's considerable power on his side than view him as a challenge or rival.

He pondered whether to tell him about Amon. Aurelius's spies had followed the Southern trader until he split away from following Flora's train and headed south, but Aurelius still felt that the man was up to something more. But no—better to leave him convinced that Rechab had run off with Alack and was not in Flora's company at all. Whatever doubts Aurelius had about that, the shepherd boy was a convenient scapegoat, and he was not eager to send Nadab into conflict with his sister. The more men of wealth and means who thought highly of him and all connected with him, the better.

Nadab began to turn away, and Aurelius put out a hand to prevent him. "Surely you are not taking your leave so soon?"

"I want to find my daughter," Nadab said.

"Perhaps I can help you," Aurelius offered. "Of late my influence has grown. I can help send out a message to those who cross the desert—to look for a shepherd boy and a trader's daughter who have fled together."

Nadab considered the offer. "Why should you go to so much trouble and expense?" he asked.

"Goodwill, my friend," Aurelius said. "And the rule of law, which is in my domain here. The boy is a subject of Bethabara and has no right to steal your daughter from you; he should be brought to justice."

The trader's face darkened. "The money he has cost me . . ."

"Justice should be done," Aurelius repeated. "Now, about the expense . . ."

"Yes, yes," Nadab said, waving his hand. "I will help you pay for messengers. I want them found."

———•◆•———

Flora left her home of twelve years before first light, alone. She said good-bye to no one, made no ceremony of her going. She had left this way many times before, going out annually to care for her business and then return. Only the Teacher knew that this time, she would not come back.

The dry air was chilled as she passed through the silent pre-dawn desert. As she crested the ridge, she looked back on the silvering river and the walls of her home one last time.

This was not how she had ever thought to end her pilgrimage.

When she reached the village closest to Essea, she put aside her sorrow and snapped into business. They all knew her here; it would not be hard to gather her usual employees and form a train of protection and help.

So she thought.

But when the eyes of Joachim, the aged fighter who had traveled with her the last fifteen years, lit on her, they widened in surprise.

"Mistress!" he burst out, keeping his voice low. "What are you doing here?"

"I've come back to take up business again," she said, wondering at his strong reaction. "It turns out I was not finished."

"But—" he stopped and composed himself. "But Mistress, I do not understand how you can be here so soon."

She lifted an eyebrow. "What do you mean, Joachim?"

"Aaron left here only yesterday in answer to your summons," Joachim said. "Has an angel carried you here from the head of the river?"

Bewildered, she sat down on the carpets in the corner of Joachim's merchant stall. "Joachim, I do not know what you are talking about. What summons? The head of the river?"

He looked around him, and ascertaining that no one in the market was listening, he lowered his voice even further. "Word came just yesterday that Aaron was to meet you at the head of the river with mules, writing materials, and arms. He left as soon as he could gather it all together."

"I still do not understand," Flora said. "I never sent such a message. The head of the river? I've been in Essea all this time."

"Nevertheless, word *did* come. From a little village a day's ride north. They said you had come alone and in disguise to the village, and nearly found yourself in trouble but revealed who you were in time. They also said you owe them money—weren't traveling with none, but left them a pledge, signed, if you please, for food and supplies given."

Flora's head swam, but only for a moment. "Rechab," she said. "It must be Rechab." She almost laughed with relief. Rechab was alive, then, and free. And traveling under her name—there was wisdom in that. Especially if she gathered protection to herself.

"Why only Aaron?" she said. "Why didn't she call for you also? Form the train properly?"

"I don't know, Mistress," Joachim said. "We thought it was you and wondered the same, but we trust your judgment."

Her mind hard at work now, Flora nodded. "Well, it's good for me she left you. I require your services, Joachim. Chiefly your sword."

"You have it, of course."

"I shall want your secrecy as well," she said. "There can't be two of us, so you are not to tell anyone who I am. Is that understood?"

His face said he did not understand at all, but he nodded anyway.

"We will travel west," Flora said, "and find others and send them to join Rechab. With arms and with funds—she can only leave so many pledges. It is the best protection I can give her."

"And what about you?" Joachim asked.

"Well, there can't be two of us abroad, can there? As far as the world knows, I am safe in Essea."

"But you won't be," Joachim bluntly pointed out.

"But I will be safe with you."

"And when you're done sending the world to join someone who isn't yourself?"

"Then I will figure out who I am," Flora said. "At this moment I'm not sure."

"And for now? What am I to call you?"

"Call me Bathsheva. Tell them I'm your wife."

The man turned red as a beet. "I can't tell them that."

She laughed. "Very well. Tell them I'm your cook. Or a nomad's wife you're delivering to her husband. Or both."

Joachim shook his head. "There is none like you, my lady."

"No one knows that better than you do, faithful friend," she said.

He coloured again. "I am your servant," he said.

She didn't contradict him, though as she considered the wrinkled face and the strong jaw, she realized anew just how faithful he was. She had brought him with her from her second husband's estate, giving him his freedom after a lifetime in thrall. He had been with her for the entirety of her career as a part-time merchant and full-time fanatic, and he had taught his fair share of bandits, raiders, and competing merchants to respect his sword arm and his unwavering loyalty.

She missed Aaron, Joachim's nephew, who had been in her service almost from toddlerhood, but was glad he had gone to serve Rechab. He took after his uncle, and Rechab would need good men around her.

The idea that someone had taken her identity—had just lifted Flora Laurentii from off of her shoulders—was heady. She would keep the Unlucky—no reason to pass that off on anyone else—but Rechab's venture had given her an unexpected freedom to decide who to be for the next little while at least, with no reason to be anyone she had been in the past.

A nomad's wife, or a cook. She laughed. Joachim looked at her, as he had been looking at her since she began proclaiming her plan, with a mixture of affection and consternation that only made her want to laugh harder.

Her plan had not been to fling herself loose on the universe, but as that was how things looked to be happening, she saw no reason not to embrace it.

———◆◆◆———

When Aaron reached Rechab three days after she sent word to him, meeting her as requested at the head of the river—only half a day's ride from the village, and in a rocky area where Rechab could shelter in a cave and live on water and the stores she had bought on credit—he greeted her with shock that she wasn't Flora.

How that message had become tangled, she didn't know. "I told them I was Flora's manager," she explained. "That I was on a mission for her, not that I was her."

"It's not your fault," he assured her. "Rumour takes on a life of its own. And not many have actually seen Flora—she rides veiled and curtained off, when she rides as a merchant and not a pilgrim. Reputation says she is very beautiful—perhaps that is why they thought you were her."

He blushed a little when he said that, reminding her of Alack. She smiled at him and took his hand. "But I am not Flora. I'm sorry to bring you here under false pretenses, but I thank you for coming to my aid. The mule and the supplies will do me a great deal of help."

"Where do you plan to go?" he asked.

At least that, she had finally decided on. She would journey south. The borders between the Sacred Land and the Southern Plains bustled with trade and market towns; she needed only to set herself up there in a shop, and she could support herself and remain anonymous. Unlike most women, she knew how to manage herself in that context. She would have to use Flora's name and credit to begin, but she could sell enough to pay off the debts from her own earnings, so she would be stealing Flora's reputation only—or so she assured herself.

She told Aaron only the surface plan. He frowned. "It is not safe," he said. "There are bandits, and slavers, not to mention the wilderness itself. You cannot go alone."

"I can't pay you to come with me," Rechab said.

"I will come. Mistress Flora would want me to."

Rechab looked away, and to her surprise, Aaron caught her chin and turned her head back. His expression was confident. "Mistress Flora would want this," he said. "She would want you safe. Perhaps even your mistaken identity is heaven's blessing on you. It is the Great

God saying that you are to use Flora's name and riches for yourself."

Or I am just stealing, Rechab wanted to say, but she didn't. His care and concern were evident, and he seemed passionately convinced that Flora would share his feelings.

He began to unload the mules, still talking to her. "I will come with you to make the journey south. You must be protected until you can build up safety of your own."

"But if I cannot pay you?" Rechab said. Her heart wanted him— needed protection, needed a friend. But it was one thing to consider paying back merchants whose goods she had bought on credit and resold; it was another thing to pay servants and bodyguards for what might be weeks or months of service. She could not doom her venture before she began.

"You will not have to," Aaron said, confident. "Mistress Flora will do it."

"But that is stealing, Aaron," Rechab said. There. She had finally let it out. "It's bad enough that I'm falsely wearing her name."

"That is the Great God's doing," Aaron said. "You did not start the rumours. The Great God blinded others to the truth so that you might be enriched. And you will not be stealing by accepting my help. It is what Mistress Flora would want me to do. If I am wrong, I will bear responsibility for it."

Relief made her knees want to buckle. What had been the prospect of a long, lonely, and dangerous journey was suddenly far more cheerful—and far more likely to succeed.

To give the mules a chance to rest, they waited two days before setting out for the south. In that time, events quickly convinced Rechab of two things: the Great God was indeed watching out for her, and Aaron had been right.

How else to explain what happened?

In the space of two days, no fewer than twenty-five men, armed and bearing provisions, supplies, and animals, arrived at the head of the river seeking her and Aaron. All said the same thing: they had been ordered to go and join Flora Laurentii at the head of the river. Ordered by Joachim, Aaron's uncle and Flora's right hand.

That she was not Flora did not seem to bother any of them overly much. They had been told that Aaron would be with her. There had also, it seemed, been some hint that this would not be a mission as usual.

So no one seemed inclined to push further.

So it was that when she set out from the caves at the head of the river, Rechab found herself embarking not as Rechab, the runaway daughter of Nadab the Trader, penniless and friendless, but as Flora Laurentii, one of the most powerful and influential women in the Sacred Land, laden with everything she needed for the journey and a full entourage of protectors and servants surrounding her. To say she was bewildered was putting it lightly.

The question of what had happened to Flora bothered her, but the growing surety that she must be behind all this comforted her worries. If Flora was masterminding a scheme of this size, and commanding all of these people in the carrying out of it, then she could not be in need of help herself.

She called Aaron to her side before they left the head of the river, early in the morning.

"Yes, Mistress?" he asked.

"I want to thank the Great God," she said. "Before we go. And to ask his blessing on our journey. But I don't know how. You spoke of him to me. Do you know what I must do to honour him?"

He seemed surprised by the question. "The chief way is to offer a sacrifice in Shalem," he said, "but Mistress Flora would sometimes gather us together to pray and bless us. To give thanks simply with words."

Rechab frowned. "Is that enough?"

"It seems the Great God smiles on it, for he always answered Mistress Flora's requests."

She nodded. "All right, then. Please gather the men together, and I will pray." Her voice shook a little. It would be strange enough doing this on her own, let alone in front of her entourage. But she was in leadership now, whether she had chosen it or not. It was only right that she formally honour the deity she had chosen to serve, and who had, it seemed, delivered her life more times than one since then.

The men gathered in a circle around her in a swath of ground that made a wide cleft in the rocks jutting up on every side. She raised her hands and tried to imagine the Great God's eye looking down upon her.

A shiver passed over her as she did.

An awareness that it was not just her imagination at work.

"I thank thee, O Great God," she said, raising her voice so it would carry, "for your goodness in preserving my life. I ask your protection and blessing now on all these good men who have come to my side."

She ought to ask blessing on Flora also, she thought, but somehow, even though all these men knew better than to believe the charade, she couldn't drop the mantle of being Flora long enough to ask a verbal blessing upon her. She would take up Flora's habit of prayer—at least once a day—and be sure to bless her friend then.

Finding she had no more words to say, she added belatedly, "Amen," and the men thundered "Amen" in response.

Heartened by the prayer, she allowed Aaron to escort her to her camel, and the journey south began.

CHAPTER 15

The tribesmen kept the crew of the ship for another three days, feeding—indeed, feasting—them and loading them with goods and honours. Kol Abaddon was honoured most of all, with the captain a close second. Alack was largely ignored, taken for a servant, if he had to guess. Kol Abaddon did nothing to correct this impression, treating Alack more or less as he always did—keeping him within arm's reach, but talking to him little and sending him for food whenever he wanted it.

Although Alack grew more glad by the day that the Great God had spared these men's lives, and he smiled at the village children who played and ran without fear around their elders, he was growing impatient and weary with the delay. Homesickness gnawed at him. He had little wish to get back on the ship, but they could not stay here forever. The sooner they reached the Westland, the sooner they could finish their business there and return to the Sacred Land. Or so he told himself.

On the third day, he excused himself from the company—not that anyone really noticed—and went to walk along the water's edge. The sea stretched out before him, brilliant blue. He could see whitecaps and swells beyond the reef, but here, between the rocks and the shore, the water was calm. He still marveled to think that the sea monster had deliberately trapped them here, where they could not help but be caught by the pirating natives. But it seemed the Great God was stronger, and smarter, than a sea monster.

His feet took him some distance up the beach, farther than he had intended to go. He had no wish to return. The men had spent their three days drinking and carousing, and Kol Abaddon was surlier than ever. The natives' food was strange to Alack and not really to his liking. He was happier wandering than remaining in their midst.

There had been no sign of others on this shore; the tribesmen appeared to be all the humanity that lived here. So Alack was unprepared to stumble across the remains of a camp.

Yet there it was. And it was not like anything he had seen the natives build. They had a peculiar way of creating a fire, and of laying out their village, and anyway, their own men would have no reason to camp so close to home. This was very different. He could see the marks of booted feet in the sandy earth; the campfires—four of them—burned not the native fuel but coal. He bent down over one of them and felt in the black ash, pulling his hand back when he found live embers.

Someone had been here only the night before, unless he missed his guess.

Suddenly on high alert, Alack rose from his crouch slowly, scanning the treeline and the water for men or a ship. Tracks led into the trees, although there were so many of them that he was not sure exactly what he was looking at—if he was seeing signs of where they had gone, or if men had simply wandered in and out of the jungle the night before, perhaps searching for food or fuel.

If nothing else, the presence of this many foreigners on these shores spelled at least potential danger. He had to go back and warn the crew, and their hosts. Right now they were all too busy feasting and celebrating their strange alliance to notice if an enemy were about to come down on their heads.

He heard the battle when he was still a distance away, and broke into a run.

He was too late.

The foreigners had indeed gone through the trees, and had come upon the village unawares.

Smoke rising met his eyes, and as his pounding feet propelled him forward, he heard screams and crying. The children. The women. The families Kol Abaddon had spared from grief and bereavement.

And shouts and the sounds of swords and shields. The men at arms.

Only yards from the fight, a sinewy arm reached out of the trees and grabbed Alack by the shoulder, hauling him off his feet and sending him sprawling from the force of his own momentum. He recognized Kol Abaddon's fierce eyes before he could make out the rest of him in the trees.

"Hist," he said. "Hide."

"But the men—"

"The fight is lost."

"But—"

Kol Abaddon's face went white, and he shoved Alack hard. He fell back into the cover of palm fronds as before his eyes, three men attacked Kol Abaddon. The fight was over before it began. If he had not been there, perhaps the prophet would have had time to gather his wits and fight, but he was too busy pushing Alack out of the way. Not that it did any good. Alack found his feet with a shout and charged to his mentor's rescue. A blow to the back of his head sent him sprawling again, and before he knew what was happening, his head was splitting and his arms were being tied behind his back.

Alack woke with his head screaming and his stomach heaving and wondered where he was. Kol Abaddon sat across from him with his hands bound and his lip split and bleeding; the side of his head was purple and swollen. Gauging from his headache, Alack doubted he looked much better.

"Where are we?" he managed to say, his voice thick and slurring. He could hardly move his mouth.

Kol Abaddon did not answer, but in the time it took to ask the question, Alack had gathered that they were in the hold of a ship. It was dark, but a little light seeped in from above. The space was cramped, just big enough to sit up in with their legs pulled toward them. Water was leaking and running down the walls. He groaned.

The sea again.

His eyes locked on Kol Abaddon and begged for some answer.

"Slavers," Kol Abaddon said.

Alack turned his head with some pain and saw that they were surrounded by other captives, mostly women and children. A few men were among them. He recognized two sailors and three of the tribesmen. If there were more, it was too dark to tell.

"They are mostly dead," Kol Abaddon said.

Alack's eyes filled with unexpected tears. Why? Why had the Great God spared their lives only to allow this? Why such a brief respite for so many of them? Was mercy always so short-lived?

"Where are they taking us?" he asked.

"Where we are meant to go. To the Westland," Kol Abaddon answered.

The messenger had watched long enough. He turned to go back to the Holy Mountain and Bethabara, as sure as he could be of the news he carried.

True, he was supposed to be looking for a woman with a young shepherd boy—and this man was anything but young. Still, the woman was right. She was veiled, but he could see she was beautiful and cultured—not the nomad's old biddy the man was trying to pass her off as. They were sufficiently poor, clearly trying to avoid questions, and going in the right direction.

It had to be Rechab. From the looks of things, the girl had run off with a lover after all—but the shepherd boy was innocent. It would not be the first time a woman had been seduced by a man twice her age.

Had he needed any extra assurance, he found it in the conversation he overheard. Coming close enough to their camp to smell the smoke from their small fire, he had heard them speaking in hushed tones of Nadab the Trader.

He turned his mule and began to ride. It would take him two days to reach the Holy Mountain. He hoped Aurelius would be happy enough with the news to pay him extra for it. To Nadab it should not matter where his daughter was found, so long as she was found, but to Aurelius, it was good news that she was not with Flora Infortunatia. Of the master's unlucky sister, the messenger also had news. He had heard rumours that she had reconvened her merchant train and was going south. All good news to Aurelius, surely. He had been a luckier man than usual of late. His sister's business partners taking up alliances with him, the king in Shalem smiling upon him, and now even the prophet gone.

Shem had heard that news just before he left. It had been weeks since the prophet troubled the people of Bethabara, and now shepherds were confirming that he had not been seen or heard in the wilderness for some time. He was gone, or dead. Either way, it was good news for Aurelius and for any who did not wish to listen to the lunatic's ravings about judgment and armies.

Shem smiled. Anyone with eyes to see knew the prophet was mad. Times had never been better for the Sacred Land, and all because they had made alliances with other nations and broadened their religious observances to other gods.

Shem himself was a worshipper of Amon-Heth, a deity of the South who ruled over deserts and warfare. He went up to the Holy City every year to pay vows and make obeisance to the Great God, and on the way out lingered at Amon-Heth's shrine to honour him as well. He had seen no reason not to do so. A man could not have too many gods on his side.

Evening was already casting long shadows over the ground, and it played tricks with his eyes as the sounds of the wild beasts stirring tweaked his nerves. The landscape here was rocky, full of slabs of granite that jutted up from the sandy earth, casting strange shadows and shielding many a hiding place. The moon was rising on the horizon, full and beautiful in a sky that was still blue. Shem's eyes darted nervously at the nearby sound of jackals—or at least, he thought it was jackals. In places like this, rumour said the goat daemons—sa'iyrs, the People called them—lurked. His father had told him stories of the sa'iyrs and how they would tear a man's heart out and eat it. He made a sign over his heart and invoked the name of Amon-Heth to protect him.

Then his mule stopped and refused to go any farther. He kicked and swore at it for a moment, but the animal only brayed and bucked and refused to go another step.

His heart suddenly filling with dread, Shem raised his eyes to the shadow-streaked line of rock slabs before him.

Something stood there. Something tall, dark, thin, but terrifying and strong.

His eyes grew wide as the form became clearer to him, seeming to form out of the shadows. Twice the height of a man, with the head of a jackal. He had seen this form many times in the shrines he visited in the Holy City and in his home village.

He stood in the presence of Amon-Heth himself.

Shaking with fear, Shem slid off his mule and went down on his knees. He wanted to avert his eyes, but he could not look away—as though the creature was controlling his gaze.

Slowly, the figure lifted its arm and pointed west. It said nothing, but Shem felt his response was desired. "Yes," he said, his voice quivering. "Yes, I will go where you say."

Just as slowly, the figure nodded.

And Shem found that without moving, he was once again seated upon his mule—and facing where the apparition had pointed.

Through his fear, a shred of elation began to work its way from his heart. He had been visited by a god, and given direction! But why? And what did this portend?

The mule was still skittish and clearly frightened, to the point that Shem found it easier to dismount and lead the animal than to try to convince it to hold a steady course. He stroked its muzzle and talked to it, calming himself down at the same time, as he walked where the god had told him to go.

At first they seemed to be journeying into nothing. But then the ground dropped away in an expected slope, covered with shale and scraggly juniper trees, and there at the base was a merchant's camp. If

Shem had any doubt or hesitation, it was erased when he saw, clearly woven into the tents, the emblems of Amon-Heth's priesthood. This was where he was meant to be.

He stumbled and slipped his way down the slope, sending a cascade of rock and sand ahead of him to announce his way. He swallowed hard as a band of armed men gathered to greet him, scimitars in hand. At first glance none of them seemed to belong to the People; they were a mix of Hill People and Southerners, marked so by their dress and hair and the amulets they wore. Now that he grew closer, he could see that some of the tents also bore the emblems of Kimash and Dargona, gods of the Hill People.

The guards waited as he finished making his ungraceful way down, his hand still on the mule's reins. They made no move to lower their weapons, but neither did they advance on him.

One of them, a tall, broad-shouldered Southerner shaved entirely bald, stepped forward.

"What do you seek?" he asked, his voice heavily accented.

"I . . ." Shem froze for a moment. What could he possibly say?

"I wish to speak with your master," he said finally.

"On what errand do you come?" the big man pressed.

"I . . . I have a message," Shem said. "It is personal, for your master only." He straightened his shoulders and tried to look confident, then compulsively made the sign of Amon-Heth over his heart again. "I come in the name of the god Amon-Heth."

The big man looked surprised, but he turned and stalked into the camp, leaving the rest of the taciturn bunch to watch over a nervous Shem. He returned minutes later and motioned for Shem to follow him.

Releasing the mule, Shem stepped gingerly past the guards, who parted to let him through, and followed the Southerner down a row of tents to one where the lord of the caravan clearly dwelt. Its outer skins, made of camel skin, were dyed rich purple and blue. The Southerner led Shem through layers of curtains made of skins, wool, and linen, all dyed and woven with designs, into an interior that smelled of spices. Oil lamps shone on the opulence of a man who lived on the merchant's road in comfort and wealth: cushions, carpets, silks, and low tables.

Behind the largest of these sat a man at meat, his table spread with wine, honeyed cakes, and various dried fruits. He too was a Southerner, with the characteristic lack of hair, light skin, and aristocratic face. He did not stand when Shem entered. As the guard stepped aside, Shem awkwardly went to his knees, bowing before his host.

"Rise," the man said. "I am told you have a message from the god Amon-Heth."

Shem's eyes flicked to the guard. He wasn't sure whether he wanted to keep his communication private, or whether he was simply embarrassed to flounder in the presence of more than one imposing man, but he did not want to speak to more than this one.

"You may go," the merchant told his servant. "This man is not a threat."

As Shem wondered how precisely the merchant knew that, the guard nodded and left. Behind the curtained walls there might be any number of others, but at least appearances were that they were alone. He relaxed slightly.

"My tale is strange," he said.

"Tell it."

"I was sent by my master to find a runaway," Shem said. "And having done so, I was traveling back to report to him when I had a . . . a vision. The great god Amon-Heth—of whom I am also a worshipper—appeared in my path, blocking my way. As I bowed before him, he pointed west—a direction which led me straight to you. But I do not know why."

"You said you have a message," the man said.

"For my master, yes."

"But perhaps our master has decided the message is for me." The man leaned forward, hands folded, smiling. "I too am in search of a runaway. And undoubtedly the god led you here. I am named for Amon-Heth—I am Amon of the Southern Plains."

Shem had heard the name before. Amon was one of the most powerful of the merchants who traded in the Holy City and thereabouts, famed for his arcane knowledge and wisdom. From what he could see, nothing of Amon's reputation had been an exaggeration.

The man's voice was hypnotic, almost a purr. The effect of it, along with his wealth and the still-fresh memory of seeing Amon-Heth on the ridge, convinced Shem that this once, it would not be wrong to share his confidence with one other than his own master. Had not a powerful deity directed this meeting?

"Who is your master?" Amon asked.

"Aurelius Florus Laurentinus," Shem said, "governor of Bethabara."

"Yes, I know him well," Amon said. "I was a guest in his house not long hence. We are allies, Aurelius and I. Now I am certain—the message you were taking to him is meant for my ears also."

And surely it must be so, Shem reasoned. A messenger who would spread his news as rumour to others was to be condemned, even punished, but this was the will of a god. And Amon's words—of alliance, and his "also"—comforted his heart.

"Then I will tell you," he said.

"Good," Amon said. He motioned to the table before him. "Come, partake as you tell your story."

"If you please," Shem said, realizing he was still on his knees and could not move gracefully to the table, "I will give my message first.

There is not a great deal to tell."

"Then let us hear it."

"My master sent me on behalf of Nadab the Trader, to find the trader's daughter—a runaway, called Rechab. At first Nadab was convinced the girl had run off with the governor's sister—one Flora Laurentii. Mayhap you know her."

"Of course," Amon said, his eyes revealing nothing. "All who trade in this region know Flora the Unlucky."

"But my master, Governor Aurelius, felt the girl had not gone off with Flora but with a lover—a boy who tends sheep. He promised Nadab to send messengers—I among them—to seek them out and bring back word of where they might be found."

"A great deal of effort, to find one runaway girl."

Shem reddened a little at the idea that any of his story was being called into question. "It is my understanding the girl is worth a great deal of money to her father. She is beautiful and was raised to be genteel; though his business is his own, most believe he has betrothed her to a man in the Holy City of great wealth and perhaps of great position."

"A not unheard-of deed," Amon said, putting Shem at his ease again. "And now you are returning to your master. Does this mean you have found them?"

"I have," Shem said, his chest swelling with pride. "But it is not quite as my master thought. Indeed, she has run away, but the man with her is old—a mercenary, I would wager."

Something jumped into the man's eyes this time; he had been unreadable until now, but for the first time Shem could see excitement in his expression. "And they are close?" he asked.

"Very close. Only an hour's ride to the south and east."

Amon clapped his hands, making Shem jump. "So the gods have

ordained it," he said. "I thank you for your faithful report. Now come, eat. I will see to it that you are well compensated for your report." Amon stood, revealing ornately embroidered robes. He paused. "Eat your fill while I go to consult with my men, and servants will tend you should you need anything. I will return and give you a message to take to the governor of Bethabara."

Unease shifted in Shem's belly—he had never lied to his master. Amon seemed to see it. "I too have an interest in this runaway," he said, "for she is more than she appears. I will give you words to speak to your master that are not lies, though they will not be the whole truth. And then, if you are willing, I will keep you in my employ, though from a distance."

Shem nodded, and Amon left the curtained chamber. Hobbling up off his knees, he went to the lavish table and sat down, slowly putting his hand to the cakes and fruit and beginning to eat. His stomach expressed his lack of ease; though he was sure he had come here for the right reasons, yet the idea of entering Amon's employ unnerved him—as did the knowledge that he had just betrayed his master's trust. But as he ate, he found himself warming to this new master. He was not, after all, hurting Aurelius. He was simply accepting a second employer—expanding his interests as any good businessman would do.

Shem helped himself to a goblet of wine and dismissed the last queasy thought that came to his mind: wondering just what Amon wanted with Rechab, and what would happen to her when he found her.

CHAPTER 16

With the falling of evening, Joachim set up camp without a word, preparing everything exactly as he had always done in Flora's employ—only without the larger retinue, the tents and luxuries, the camels and mules. He set up a single tent where Flora could sleep and started a fire and pottage to cooking over it, and he knew the exact moment when Flora would wander to the edges of their little encampment and pray.

In the twelve years since she joined the community at Essea, she had never once missed a time of prayer. Even before then she had been devout. Flora chose all her servants carefully, traveling only with those who feared the Great God and worshipped no other idols, but none was so pious as she. The old man sat back as she walked off so he could keep an eye on her. After all these years he could pray the prayers along with her, sing the songs, intone the supplications. He did not. He simply let his heart resonate with the snatches he could hear from this distance, and he honoured her.

Flora covered her face as she began the prayers, singing lightly through her fingers. The melody was sad and sweet, a minor key, one of the first songs she had learned in the desert. She sang in the language of the People: the evening song, welcoming in the night and giving it into the Great God's hands with thanks and also with lament. For every day was a day of blessing, and every day was a day of sorrow—especially as long as the People's hearts remained cold to their Creator.

She had sung the words so many times that now, they sang themselves. They held meaning only if she concentrated on them. And tonight, in spite of herself, she couldn't.

Instead her mind ranged over the wilderness. Back to the desert community, her home no more. Back to Rechab, traveling under her name and hopefully with her retinue. Back to Bethabara and her sly half-brother, and back to the past—to childhood, to their mother, to the idol of Kimash, to fear.

All that seemed equally distant in this moment.

In this moment, Flora did not know who she was anymore. To this point her life had always led somewhere, and now she no longer knew where it was leading.

She finished the evening song and lowered her hands, watching as the sun sank over the desert sands. A full moon already graced the sky, and the first bright stars. Though they were not yet visible, she knew the constellations behind them, the whole canopy and story of the heavens that would unfold with the darkness. Automatically she began the next prayer, but it died on her tongue.

She stood in silence, watching the change from day to night, from blue sky to black, from empty heavens to tapestry.

Who am I? She asked silently. And what is my part in this story? It startled her to realize that in the quiet of her mind, she had asked the questions in the tongue of her childhood—in the language of the Hill People, themselves abominations to the Great God. And yet that was the crux of her role in this story, wasn't it? That she ought not to be accepted, and yet she had been; that she had taken devotion to the limits of where she was allowed to go, and she could not turn away—her whole heart was here. But if she had truly reached the borders of the Great God's favour . . . if she had been, in the end, cast out . . .

She laughed, but bitterly, to think of Joachim not far away, watching her pray. Not praying himself, not availing himself of the favour that belonged naturally to every one of the Holy People because they had been chosen. She would give anything to have the access he had. To have rights to enter the temple, to have the assurance of the Great God's unchanging, covenantal faithfulness.

Even as she thought it, a rush of darkness came over her, staggering her on her feet. For a split second she saw a mass of roiling dust on an evening horizon, the unnatural cloud of thousands of marching feet.

Kol Abaddon's coming army.

The dark side of covenant with any god who cared was retribution. Or in this case, judgment.

It was the reason Flora had run to the Great God in the first place. The reason she trusted him, the reason she worshipped him, the reason she would never give her heart to any other deity. Because while other gods made bloodthirsty demands and accepted bribes, and lashed out in cruel and often petty ways when displeased, the Great God had drawn his people into a covenant with justice at its heart. Flora's Hill People kinfolk were barred from the temple for a thousand generations because they had stabbed the Holy People in the back when once they were allies. The God's laws demanded honesty, loyalty, goodness.

And where the People allowed a breach to open in justice, the Great God himself would come to close it.

She thought the vision had lasted only a moment, but when it passed, she heard Joachim shouting behind her, and the sounds of a scuffle. She turned, still dizzy with the effects of what she had seen, to see three men creeping up behind her, swords drawn.

They were too close, and she was unarmed. She raised her hands to show surrender, watching warily as they approached. Two of them lowered their swords and took her elbows, propelling her back toward the camp without a word. There, six others waited, standing around Joachim. The old man was bound and bloodied and on his knees, but alive. A quick glance told her most of these men were Southerners, and likely not bandits—they were too groomed, too orderly. Without saying a single word, they hauled Joachim to his feet, renewed their grip on Flora's elbows, and began a forced march away from the encampment. Two of the men stayed behind to tear down the tent and take anything they could find.

"I'm sorry, Mistress," Joachim mumbled through a bloody mouth; one of the men cuffed him in the back of the head, nearly knocking him off his feet. Flora managed a terse smile and nod, trying to communicate through her eyes that she did not blame him. But this was real trouble, and she could not remove fear from her expression. For a wild moment she had considered declaring who she was and promising these men rich reward if they would let her go, but the foolishness of that plan presented itself to her immediately. Whoever they were, identifying herself would only give them reason to hold her hostage.

And besides, there was Rechab to think of. Rechab was Flora Laurentii now, and Flora was determined that she would remain in that role as long as she needed it.

Or, depending on what was about to happen to her, perhaps forever.

The journey on foot ended at a stream not far away, where still more men waited with camels. These exchanged a few words with their captors in the Southern tongue, but too quietly for Flora to hear—she had picked up enough of the language in her years of commerce that she might have understood them. Once again she considered asserting herself, and once again decided against it. Docility was hardly her usual way, but anything else at the moment was asking for trouble—for herself and for Joachim.

She mounted a camel with the help of one of the men, who climbed up behind her and held her tight around the waist. She pulled her veil more securely against her and checked for weapons within reach. There—a broad curved knife hung from the saddle, where she could grab it if she maneuvered correctly and fast enough. Likewise, she might be able to pull out the blade the man wore in his sash, tucked against his hip. He motioned for her to sit still, and she did, hoping he had taken her fidgeting for a lady's natural fear. She looked for Joachim but could no longer see him; he was riding somewhere to the rear of the train.

The journey across the sands took an hour. As they rode, the stars appeared, spreading themselves against the sky in a dazzling display. Flora searched them out, all the old stories, the old figures. Here, the running figure of Isha was especially clear. She almost smiled. She had often wondered where Isha was running, and whether she ran from or ran to. Tonight, she might be the woman in the stars herself. And yet she still didn't know the answer to those questions.

The camels crossed a series of ridges and passed through a field of jagged rock slabs, and at last they came down into a gentle valley where a trader's encampment lay. It was dark but for the light of a few fires, and shadowy figures ringed the boundaries of the camp, tall, broad, and imposing. She had read these men aright, then: they were not bandits, but the well-trained and well-paid emissaries of a man of means and power.

That might mean her chances of living through the night had been raised. But she felt it would be simpler to deal with bandits.

The man behind her called out a greeting to the shadowy guards, and they passed directly into the camp, stopping to dismount only a few feet within the silhouetted tents. Her captor slipped off and raised his hands to help her. She paused, then swung her leg over in what was guaranteed to cause an awkward half-fall.

He caught her, as she knew he would. And she had just enough time in the scramble to grab the blade from the saddle and hide it beneath her veil. The man muttered curses in the Southern tongue, but he had not seen her. She smiled to herself as he motioned her forward, toward an imposing tent. Eyes were on her, but she could not see their owners; servants or guards or slaves, hiding in the shadows and behind curtains and veils. The silence here was not silent; it was full of whispers and furtive movement. And fear.

The fear troubled her.

She passed into the dark interior of the tent and found it dimly lit by oil lamps that burned low. She stood alone in the midst of it, and she gripped the hilt of the knife and waited.

A figure entered. A man she knew at once.

"I wish you to remove your veil," Amon the Southern Trader instructed her.

She did not move.

In a position of power, surrounded by men she trusted and buttressed by the wealth at her fingertips, Flora was more than Amon's match. But here—in his own camp—entirely under his power. Here, he was the last man she wanted to face.

And she realized that he did not yet know who she was.

She gripped the knife harder and wondered if she could possibly overpower the man—and maintain her advantage against all the wrath she would surely call down on her head in the act of doing so.

"I said, I wish you to remove your veil. You will do as I say, girl."

Girl.

No, he did not know who she was.

But there was nothing for it. She could not attack him and win, and he would not allow her to disobey any longer.

Reaching up to draw the veil aside, she said, "Is this any way to greet an old partner, Amon?"

She saw it in his eyes—the shock, quickly lidded again. He'd had no idea who was in his camp.

But then why go to the trouble to bring her here?

"Flora," he said.

"It seems I am a surprise to you," Flora said. "Just who did you think you had kidnapped?"

He didn't answer that, although the expression in his eyes conceded that she had won some sort of victory—in catching him so off guard, at least. At the same time, his lidded gaze did nothing to hide the fact that he was calculating now. His trap hadn't been set for her, but it had caught her regardless, and the value of his prize could not fail to occur to him.

Had he been a man of honour, she might have been safe. But few traders were men of honour, and Amon less than most. Their actions were governed by advantage, not principle, and though Amon was known for his worship and knowledge in the many religions of the region, yet his highest god was Mammon.

The one god by whom Flora found herself unusually favoured.

Amon began to pace, uncannily like a tiger, his hands clasped behind his back.

"The man with you—one of your servants?"

"Yes," she said. "You will not harm him."

He chuckled. "I have no plans to do so. But you, Lady Infortunatia, are not in a position to tell me what I will or will not do—or do I really need to point that out?"

"You can set your price," Flora said. "I will see that it is paid."

He stopped pacing. "Yes, it is a high ransom you can offer, is it not? But what if I should decide you are worth more captive than free?"

"Captive, I will order none of my resources allocated to you. And those who manage them will give up nothing simply because you tell them to. Even my death is to their advantage; everything I own is assigned to those who manage it after my death. So my word is the only power you have."

She wondered if that disappointed or surprised him—he was veiling his expression too well to tell. But there was no bluff in her words.

"That arrangement seems less than wise," he said. "Would it not make it a little too tempting for your servants to arrange for your death?"

Flora knew the practice of the Southern Plains—kill all a man's servants when he died and bury them in a tomb alongside him, along with much of his wealth. It made servants loyal and fiercely protective. And it turned her stomach.

"Some of us prefer to deal in honour and loyalty than to traffic in fear and death," she said.

His eyes flicked down. "In the same sort of honour that has you planning to attack me? I am not blind to what you are holding."

She sighed imperceptibly and let her veil drop away from her hand and the blade she held. "Any woman knows the advantage of self-defense," she said. "After all, it was one of your servants who attacked me in the dead of night, in my own hut, in Essea. Or do you deny that?"

"I do not," he said. "But I deny your implication—that I ordered the attack. What benefit would that be to me?"

"That, I cannot say. But I do not know what advantage it is to you to have a traveling woman and her bodyguard brought to you in the midst of the wilderness, or why you pursued Rechab such a distance across the desert—why you pursued her at all. What are you doing, Amon? You do nothing without cause and nothing that will not benefit you. But your actions of late are a mystery to me."

His eyes gleamed at that. He motioned to the cushions in one corner of the tent floor. "Come, sit," he said. "Put the knife down first."

Reluctantly, she did as he said, crouching and placing the knife on the ground. He was already seating himself amidst the cushions, and she took her seat beside him, as she had done before many times—but always as trader to trader, never as captive to captor. She liked this balance of power considerably less.

"You observed the stars as you came into my camp," Amon said as she seated herself.

"Indeed."

"And did you read them? Does your knowledge extend to the skies, or does your blind loyalty to a single deity keep you ignorant of what the stars portend?"

She stiffened. "The Great God is lord over the skies, and he uses them to speak as he will."

"Yet he denies his people the right to ask of the stars and to worship before them."

"He reserves all worship to himself, as is right and good."

Amon laughed, and her face burned. "It is good for the People that they have left such stricture behind."

"Not all have done so."

"Your singular devotion has always been admirable in its way. But you know yourself how rare such devotion is. Most of the People do as all wise men do—seek and worship whatever god will aid them in their need."

Flora did not answer, waiting for him to come back to whatever he'd intended to reveal.

He did not disappoint. "Could you read the stars," he said, "you might have seen what those who are wise all know: that the star of Kimash is ascendant. The god of the Hill People rises to bestow great favour and wealth on all who will seek him in the coming season."

"The abomination of my mother's people," Flora said. "When did Kimash ever possess wealth or favour to give? The Hill People scrape and scrabble in a barren country, thieving and slaving. And you wish to attract the favour of their god?"

"Seasons turn and change," Amon said. "So it is that the Holy People were once great and strong, but now serve as a whore for other nations mightier and stronger than they. So it is that the people of the Southern Plains were once greater than all, but now have diminished. Some rise, some fall. The stars tell us who will come next to power and whose doom awaits."

"And you trust that you speak their language," Flora said.

He smiled indulgently. "It is not the stars alone that speak. You have already encountered my slave—"

"A pitiful wretch," Flora interrupted, "enslaved by an evil spirit."

"A spirit of prophecy," Amon corrected, "one that speaks for Kimash. You have wondered, no doubt, why I keep him in my retinue. It is because I, unlike you, value the voices of the gods. As many of them as I can gather to myself."

Flora laughed bitterly. "All but the voice of the one god who speaks true. You have paid no heed to the voice of the prophet in the wilderness."

"The madman who speaks of coming judgment?" Amon said. "I have heard his ravings and found them worthless. The stars say nothing of the army he claims will soon march upon the land and conquer it. To heed his warnings would be folly and loss to us all."

"To ignore them may mean death. He has seen a great army overrunning the Holy City; do you imagine its conquests will end there? You too are in danger, Amon."

"And you?" Amon said. "How did you intend to escape the coming wrath? Did you imagine to hide out in Essea, in that god-forsaken stretch of desert? But if I am not mistaken, they have cast you off."

Anger tightened her stomach. *Because of you*, she wanted to say. *If you had not hunted down Rechab, I would still have a home.*

Rechab.

Suddenly she understood why she was here.

"But you did not mean to catch me out in the desert," Flora said, her voice mounting up in confidence. "You have been hunting a woman, and you believed me to be her. Why are you looking for Rechab, Amon? She is nothing—a trader's daughter. Worth money to him, but nothing worth chasing halfway across the wilderness."

"She would be what you say," Amon said, "if Kimash had not marked her."

Flora's blood ran cold. Of course—the slave whose "prophecies" Amon valued. It had all begun with his pronouncement in Bethabara that Rechab had been sold to the gods of the Hills. But that still did not explain Amon's fixation on hunting the girl down.

"When a god's star is in the ascendant," Amon told her, "there are signs on the earth below. His priests gather and sacrifice. The god's power is consolidated and his allies identified. Kimash's star is no small wonder. The season that comes is no ordinary season. Even now his power grows in the place he has chosen, and with it his wealth and influence. None may run when he has chosen them. None may escape the reach of his arm."

Flora drew back as Amon spoke—his visage seemed lit by his words, and what she saw there frightened her. As though the man had been possessed by a little of what afflicted his slave.

"So you think to be rewarded by bringing Rechab to the god," Flora said.

"I will show my devotion," Amon said. "I trust the Rising One to honour that."

"But you cannot," Flora heard herself saying, even as she inwardly wrestled between discretion and triumph, "because you have not found her after all. She has slipped from your grasp every time you have tried to take her captive. So you will go empty-handed to show your devotion."

For the first time, anger appeared in his countenance. He did not move, yet she felt menaced—physically threatened. "Not empty-handed," he said. "The chase has not ended. And the gods did not lead me to Rechab, but they did lead me to you. Do not expect me to overlook that."

She stood, turned her back, and walked several steps away from him. Her heart pounded as she did so; she knew she had no power here, that any dignity she pretended to was a flimsy sham. That turning her back could get her killed just as easily as it could keep her alive. But for the moment she had to assert some strength—had to show that she was not simply powerless and in his grasp. "So what then is my status here?" she asked, not turning back to him.

His voice behind her was calm. "You are my prisoner," he said. "Further than that, I will tell you once I have sought the gods and decided whether you should know their will."

"And you will not harm my servant."

"He is no use to me dead."

She nodded. It was the best she could do. She heard the rustling of him rising from the cushions, and then he was standing right behind her—unnervingly close.

"I will leave you here," he said. "The tent is well guarded. You may use any portion of it, but you may not leave. You will be told when we are ready to move camp and will be escorted at that time. I will send you food and drink and whatever else is necessary."

She nodded.

He left.

Before her eyes, in the shadowy light of the oil lamp, a shape took form before her eyes. It had been there all along—woven into the inner lining of the tent. But she had not seen it until now. Fear struck at her heart as she recognized it—the two-headed figure of a man, with the faces of a man on one side and a dragon on the other.

Kimash.

She sank slowly down in the cushions, unable to tear her eyes away. Thrown out of her home in the Great God, captured by her enemies—had she truly been thrown back out to the power of the one being she dreaded most?

Her heart said a prayer for protection. Tonight she would sleep in the tents of the enemy.

What tomorrow would bring remained to be seen.

CHAPTER 17

In his grand home in the city of Bethabara, Nadab the Trader quivered in fear.

"You have not delivered what you promised," the man before him said.

"I told you, Gracious Lord," Nadab said, his voice trembling, "she has run away. I am doing all in my power to seek her out, but . . ."

"The master is not a patient man," the visitor continued. His servants, all of them armed with curved scimitars that glimmered wickedly in the light, lined the walls of the receiving room. Like the man before him, each wore black robes and covered most of his face in a black scarf and turban, revealing only dark, threatening eyes.

"I was deceived by others," Nadab said. "By the governor's sister—Flora Laurentii. And a shepherd boy who goes about with the prophet in the wilderness."

"Prophet," the man said. "A charlatan. A liar. We will see him dead. It will please the master."

Nadab decided not to mention that the prophet had disappeared. No reason to add to the their anger—or to the threat looming over his head.

They had come in the night, without warning and without anyone to stay them. They slew Nadab's guards where they stood, moving so quickly and silently that no alarm was raised. And now he stood before them, helpless, a sword all but lifted above his head.

He had bowed low before the god Mammon when he offered his daughter in marriage to the high priest of Kimash. And now Mammon had come to exact a high price.

"Please," he continued, "give me more time. Even now messengers are searching the wilderness for Rechab. When they find her, they will bring her to me and she will be brought to your master without delay. I swear it will be so."

The man before him fixed cruel eyes on his face. "You know the penalty for defrauding a god."

"But I have not done so!" Nadab burst out. His knees beneath him wanted to give way, to send him toppling to the earth. "I swear the girl's disappearance has nothing to do with me. I have been deceived as you have been. Look to the enemies of your god if you would find the thieves—to Flora Laurentii and to Kol Abaddon, the mad prophet. They are the masterminds who stole her away."

From some other part of his house, he could hear sudden cries and groans. The man before him turned his head to take in the sounds and then fixed his gaze on Nadab once more. "To remind you of the price that Kimash demands, we are culling your household for you tonight. Only one will be left you alive. I trust you have wealth enough to recover from this?"

Nadab nearly choked, but he managed to say, "Yes, Gracious Lord."

"Good," the man said. "Then on the morrow, you will embark on your own journey to find your daughter and bring her back to us. If we hear that there has been any delay, we will visit you again and take the bride price from your own skin. Do you understand?"

"Yes, yes," Nadab said, tears welling up in his eyes. Tears of fear, tears of grief. The servants in his household had served him for decades. He only hoped the killings were fast and merciful.

———•◆•———

Aurelius received word from a breathless messenger boy only hours after dawn.

"Nadab the Trader found me in the market and demanded I give you this," the boy said. "He said it was urgent." Aurelius reached out to take the message, but the boy's hand was shaking, and he did not release it. His eyes were wide. "I went by his house," the child blurted. "They're all dead, my lord!"

Aurelius started, pulling his hand back. "Dead? What do you mean?"

"The gates are open and the guards and the servants—everyone dead. Even the animals. Lying out in the courtyard like they've been in a battle."

His white face gave Aurelius to know that though the boy might have some of his facts wrong, he was not lying. He reached out and snatched the note away from the lad, reading it quickly and feeling the blood drain from his own face. Forcing himself to stay calm, he reached out and put his arm around the boy's shoulders, steering him inside.

"Go and find a piece of bread for yourself," he said. "My servants will feed you; tell them I have said so. Sit. Calm yourself. And say nothing of what you have seen. All will know soon enough—but do not speak of it yet."

The boy nodded and went off in the direction Aurelius had indicated. The governor called for two of his guards.

"Go to the house of Nadab the Trader," he said. "Search the house and yard and return to tell me what you have found—everything you have found. I do not believe any will stop you."

They looked at him questioningly. He fought to keep himself calm and clearly in command. "I believe death awaits," he said. "But I must have the story confirmed. Find what has happened there, and return without telling anyone else."

They left, and he searched out Marah quickly. She was reclining in the garden, but she sat up immediately when she saw Aurelius's face.

"What is it?" she asked.

"We are under an attack," he said. "A curse."

"What are you going on about?"

"Nadab the Trader has brought evil into our midst," Aurelius said. Her impatient expression jolted him to keep going. "He sold his daughter to Kimash—to be married to the high priest in Shalem. And now the high priest has sent his servants to collect her. They murdered all of Nadab's household in the night, and Nadab himself is gone off with the morning to try to find her."

He sat down on the garden bench with a groan and buried his face in his hands. "What do I do now, fair wife? An entire household murdered—and on my watch. I cannot bring the killers to justice; they are gone. And they are the hands of Kimash. This will fall on my head."

"Perhaps not," Marah said. "You have favour at court; use it."

"What do you mean?" he asked.

"Do what you can to manage the situation here," she said, "and then go to Shalem as soon as you can and seek audience with the king. He will hear your side of this story."

"Kimash and his priests have great influence at court."

"But not the only influence; not yet. Shalem is still a city of competing interests. Be one of the first to make your case and the first to win the king to your side. You have no other choice, my husband."

She was right. He would go to Shalem and do all he could to manage this situation from there.

It was the only hope he had.

Epilogue

The Teacher stood in the desert night and gazed up at the stars. He had not slept since sending Flora away. Something had gone out of Essea with her—a spirit, a life. Its absence surprised and shook him.

Years ago he had stood here with a young man who would one day lose his family in a tragic miscarriage of justice, and who would roam in the wilderness and see visions and begin to call himself the voice of destruction. That young man had pointed to the stars.

"Do you see it?" he had asked.

The Teacher did. Isha, the Beloved, fleeing across the sky as she had done for a thousand years. But now the stars had shifted, and she ran to the Dragon—to her destruction, said Kol Abaddon.

A soft wind blew over the sands. The eye of the Dragon, the star Kimash, twinkled.

When the Southern trader had come and told him that the girl Rechab belonged to Kimash, the Teacher had thought of the stars and known he could not defend the community if Kimash came against them. The wickedness that was the Hill People's abominable god was bloodthirsty and growing in power; he could not stay it. Amon had offered to take the girl away and return her to her father, where she rightly belonged.

In his fear, the Teacher had agreed it was best.

Now he wondered if he had not thrown her, and Flora too, to the Dragon.

He wondered if there was any way they could all avoid being swallowed.

Kol Abaddon, were he here, would say no. Destruction was coming. Destruction was inevitable. The Great God had spoken from on high against his wayward, unjust, treacherous people.

The Teacher wondered where the prophet was now, and if he had changed his message at all.

But he trembled as he thought on his own betrayal of one who trusted him, and of the way the Great God's presence seemed to have removed from Essea.

They were the last of the faithful. If the Great God would no longer turn his eye on them, what hope did anyone have?

The story continues in *Comes the Dragon,*
Book 2 of The Prophet Trilogy

Rachel Starr Thomson

Rachel would love to hear from you!

You can visit her and interact online:
Web: www.rachelstarrthomson.com
Facebook: www.facebook.com/RachelStarrThomsonWriter
Twitter: @writerstarr

THE SEVENTH WORLD TRILOGY

Worlds Unseen   Burning Light   Coming Day

For five hundred years the Seventh World has been ruled by a tyrannical empire—and the mysterious Order of the Spider that hides in its shadow. History and truth are deliberately buried, the beauty and treachery of the past remembered only by wandering Gypsies, persecuted scholars, and a few unusual seekers. But the past matters, as Maggie Sheffield soon finds out. It matters because its forces will soon return and claim lordship over her world, for good or evil.

The Seventh World Trilogy is an epic fantasy, beautiful, terrifying, pointing to the realities just beyond the world we see.

"An excellent read, solidly recommended for fantasy readers."

– Midwest Book Review

"A wonderfully realistic fantasy world. Recommended."

– Jill Williamson, Christy-Award-Winning Author
of *By Darkness Hid*

"Epic, beautiful, well-written fantasy that sings of Christian truth."

– Rael, reader

Available everywhere online or special order from your local bookstore.

THE ONENESS CYCLE

  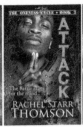  

Exile   Hive   Attack   Renegade   Rise

The supernatural entity called the Oneness holds the world together.
What happens if it falls apart?

In a world where the Oneness exists, nothing looks the same. Dead men walk. Demons prowl the air. Old friends peel back their mundane masks and prove as supernatural as angels. But after centuries of battling demons and the corrupting powers of the world, the Oneness is under a new threat—its greatest threat. Because this time, the threat comes from within.

Fast-paced contemporary fantasy.

"Plot twists and lots of edge-of-your-seat action,
I had a hard time putting it down!"

—Alexis

"Finally! The kind of fiction I've been waiting for my whole life!"
—Mercy Hope, FaithTalks.com

"I sped through this short, fast-paced novel, pleased by the well-drawn characters and the surprising plot. Thomson has done a great job of portraying difficult emotional journeys . . . Read it!"

—Phyllis Wheeler, The Christian Fantasy Review

Available everywhere online or special order from your local bookstore.

TAERITH

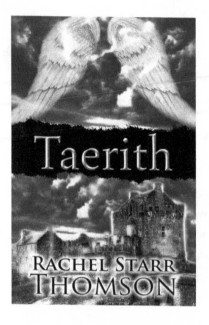

When he rescues a young woman named Lilia from bandits, Taerith Romany is caught in a web of loyalties: Lilia is the future queen of a spoiled king, and though Taerith is not allowed to love her, neither he can bring himself to leave her without a friend. Their lives soon inter-twine with the fiercely proud slave girl, Mirian, whose tragic past and wild beauty make her the target of the king's unscrupulous brother.

The king's rule is only a knife's edge from slipping—and when it does, all three will be put to the ultimate test. In a land of fog and fens, unicorns and wild men, Taerith stands at the crossroads of good and evil, where men are vanquished by their own obsessions or saved by faith in higher things.

"Devastatingly beautiful . . . I am amazed at every chapter how deeply you've caused us to care for these characters."
—Gabi

"Deeply satisfying." —Kapezia

"Rachel Starr Thomson is an artist, and every chapter of Taerith is like a painting . . . beautiful."
—Brittany Simmons

ANGEL IN THE WOODS

Hawk is a would-be hero in search of a giant to kill or a maiden to save. The trouble is, when he finds them, there are forty-some maidens— and they call their giant "the Angel." Before he knows what's happening, Hawk is swept into the heart of a patchwork family and all of its mysteries, carried away by their camaraderie— and falling quickly in love.

But the outside world cannot be kept at bay forever. Suspecting the Giant of hiding a treasure, the wealthy and influential Widow Brawnlyn sets out to tear the family apart and bring the Giant to destruction any way she can. And her two principle weapons are Hawk—and the truth.

Caught between the terrible truths he discovers about the family's past and the unalterable fact that he has come to love them, Hawk must face his fears and overcome his flaws if he is to rescue the Angel in the woods.

"A beautiful tale of finding oneself, honor and heroism; a story I will not soon forget." — Szoch

"The more I think about it, the more truth and beauty I find in the story." —H. A. Titus

Available everywhere online or special order from your local bookstore.

REAP THE WHIRLWIND

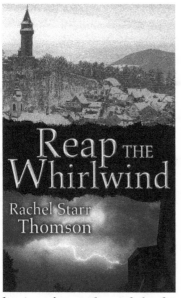

Beren is a city in constant unrest: ruled by a ruthless upper class and harried by a band of rebels who want change. Its one certainty is that the two sides do not, and will not, meet.

But children know little of sides or politics, and Anna and Kyara—a princess and a peasant girl—let their chance meeting grow into a deep friendship. Until the day Kyara's family is slaughtered by Anna's people, and the friendship comes to an abrupt end.

Years later, Kyara is a rebel—bitter, hard, and violent. Anna's efforts to fight the political system she belongs to avail little. Neither is a child anymore—but neither has ever forgotten the power of their long-ago friendship. When a secret plot brings the rebellion to a fiery head, both young women know it is too late to save the land they love.

But is it too late to save each other?

Available everywhere online.

LADY MOON

When Celine meets Tomas, they are in a cavern on the moon where she has been languishing for thirty days after being banished by her evil uncle for throwing a scrub brush at his head. Tomas is a charming and eccentric Immortal, hanging out on the moon because he's procrastinating his destiny—meeting, and defeating, Celine's uncle.

A pair of magic rings send them back to earth, where Celine insists on returning home and is promptly thrown into the dungeon. Her uncle, Ignus Umbria, is up to no good, and his latest caper threatens to devour the whole countryside. He doesn't want Celine getting in the way. More than that, he wants to force Tomas into a confrontation—and Tomas, who has fallen in love with Celine, cannot procrastinate any longer.

Lady Moon is a fast-paced, humorous adventure in a world populated by mad magicians, walking rosebushes, thieving scullery maids, and other improbable things. And of course, the most improbable—and magical—thing of all: true love.

"Celine's sarcastic 'languishing' immediately put me in mind of Patricia C. Wrede's Dealing with Dragons series—a fairy tale that gently makes fun of the usual fairy tale tropes. And once again, Rachel Starr Thomson doesn't disappoint."

— H. A. Titus

"Funny and quirky fantasy."

Available everywhere online.

THE PROPHET TRILOGY

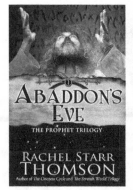  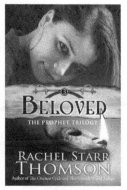

Abaddon's Eve   Comes the Dragon   Beloved

A prophet and his apprentice.
A runaway and a wealthy widow marked as an outcast.

They alone can see the terrible judgment
marching on their land.

But can they do anything to stop it?

The Prophet Trilogy is a fantasy set in
a near-historical world of deserts, temples,
and spiritual forces that vie
for the hearts of men.

Available everywhere online or special order from your local bookstore.

Short Fiction by Rachel Starr Thomson

BUTTERFLIES DANCING

FALLEN STAR

OF MEN AND BONES

OGRES IS

JOURNEY

MAGDALENE

THE CITY CAME CREEPING

WAYFARER'S DREAM

WAR WITH THE MUSE

SHIELDS OF THE EARTH

And more!

Available as downloads for
Kindle, Kobo, Nook, iPad, and more!